MW01127685

Two Journeys to the
AFTERLIFE

T. Ralph Turner

CROSSBOOKS
PUBLISHING

CrossBooks™
A Division of LifeWay
1663 Liberty Drive
Bloomington, IN 47403
www.crossbooks.com
Phone: 1-866-879-0502

First published by CrossBooks 8/22/2011

ISBN: 978-1-4627-0592-4 (sc)
ISBN: 978-1-4627-0594-8 (hc)

Library of Congress Control Number: 2011914692

Printed in the United States of America

This book is printed on acid-free paper.

Any people depicted in stock imagery provided by Thinkstock are models,
and such images are being used for illustrative purposes only.

Certain stock imagery © Thinkstock.

Also by T. Ralph Turner

How to Overcome Cooldown and Keep the Fires Burning—Hunter Books
Preparing Your Heart to Survive in a Dangerous World—Publish America
Threat Awareness—Publish America
Color Coded Motorcycle Safety—Publish America
Citizen Warrior—Wolfhunter Chronicles EBook Publishing

To my wife Joan
Without her dedication to and support of these projects, none would
have been possible.

To my wife Joan
Without her dedication to and support of these projects, none would
have been possible.

Base Scripture

THERE WAS A RICH MAN who was dressed in purple and fine linen and lived in luxury every day. At his gate was laid a beggar named Lazarus, covered with sores and longing to eat what fell from the rich man's table. Even the dogs came and licked his sores. The time came when the beggar died and the angels carried him to Abraham's side. The rich man also died and was buried. In hell, where he was in torment, he looked up and saw Abraham far away, with Lazarus by his side. So he called to him, "Father Abraham, have pity on me and send Lazarus to dip the tip of his finger in water and cool my tongue, because I am in agony in this fire." But Abraham replied, "Son, remember that in your lifetime you received your good things, while Lazarus received bad things, but now he is comforted here and you are in agony. And besides all this, between us and you a great chasm has been fixed, so that those who want to go from here to you cannot, nor can anyone cross over from there to us." He answered, "Then I beg you, father, send Lazarus to my father's house, for I have five brothers. Let him warn them, so that they will not also come to this place of torment." Abraham replied, "They have Moses and the Prophets; let them listen to them." "No, father Abraham," he said, "but if someone from the dead goes to them, they will repent." He said to him, "If they do not listen to Moses and the Prophets, they will not be convinced even if someone rises from the dead."

Luke 16: 19–31 NIV

Meet Ed Williams

Ed's Life Begins

JESSE WILLIAMS PACED BACK AND forth in the front yard of the family farmhouse. He would change directions, spinning on the heel of his cowboy boots at one edge of the porch and then head for the other edge. With each spin, his rather long black hair would lag slightly behind the change in direction of the rest of his 6 foot 4 inch frame. With each pass by the front door, his dark eyes would flick toward the opening to see if there was any sign. And with each pass, he would grow more impatient. "What are they doing?" he snapped at no one in particular, although there were several more in attendance.

After about a dozen or so of these passes, his father, sitting in the cane bottom rocking chair on the porch, spoke. His words were carefully chosen, and spoken with deliberation. His pointed way of speaking came from his Native American heritage as well as his time as an army colonel, riding with Teddy Roosevelt's Rough Riders. "Settle down, boy! How many brothers and sisters do you have?"

Jessie was in no mood for riddles. "What difference does that make, Dad?"

"How many?" the old man repeated.

Without even pausing in his journey, Jessie shot back, "Eight brothers and three sisters. So what?"

"That means that I have been where you are eleven times. This is your first. And you ain't gonna die! And neither is Janie. Your mother is

1

in there with her, and so is Aunt Ethel, the best midwife in the state. So just relax."

But the old man was wrong. Jesse snapped back at him. "Yea, Dad. You and Mom had a whole bunch of us kids. But how many did you have to bury before you even had the chance to meet them."

Jesse's dad, Amos, pulled up short in his remarks. He had plumb forgotten that. Now he remembered how hurt his son and his young wife had been at the loss of the two other babies. "Sorry, Son!" he said. "I didn't mean anything by what I said. It's just that you get so steamed up over things you can't control. And believe me, this is one thing that is totally in the hands of the Lord. You know that, and you know Him. Just leave this in His hands, and take whatever happens as His will."

Jesse felt a twinge of resentment touch his heart. He knew there was no way he could blame God for the other two or with whatever happened here. This was the first time Janie had been able to carry a child to full term. He remembered her mental state for several months after the other two. The last one was worse and lasted longer than the first. He just didn't know if she could handle another loss. They both wanted this baby more than anyone could know. So, of course, Jesse was anxious, scared, and more than a little bit short tempered when told to just relax and not worry. He knew he should leave the entire thing in God's hands, but that was easier said than done.

Then, on what he knew must be the hundredth trip back and forth between one end of the porch to the other, it happened. He heard it faintly at first. Then louder! The distinctive cry of a baby! And one with good lungs from the sound of it. Jesse's mother burst out the front door, shoving it hard enough for it to bang against the doorstop. "It's a boy!" she shouted.

Jesse began to dance around the front yard, kicking up dust. The old man fairly skipped down the steps off the porch, yelling at Jesse, "See, I told you so. God had already let me know this one was going to make it okay. See … I told you!" He continued dancing right into the yard, joining the dance with his son. "See!" he yelled again. "I told you it would all work out this time. I heard it from a good source. The Lord promised me He would hear my prayer that this baby be not only born but born healthy."

"Okay, Dad! I heard you! Praise God!" And the dust flew higher!

With that, Jesse ran into the house, through the living room, and into the bedroom, where Janie was. She looked beautiful, though exhausted. And there in her arms, all snuggled in a blue blanket, was the most fabulous gift a man could receive. A girl would have been wonderful, but a son ... wow! Jesse paused beside the bed, just looking at the tiny figure. "Thank you, Jesus! And forgive me for doubting."

"How do you like him?" Janie asked in a low voice.

Jesse sat on the edge of the bed. "My heart just isn't big enough to contain the words, Janie. I just want to run through the woods yelling at all the critters about him."

Janie spoke. "Jesse, meet Edward Ralph Williams. Edward Ralph Williams, meet your daddy." Life was wonderful beyond words.

And thus was Edward Ralph Williams introduced to the world on March 5, 1923. He was born on the Williams family farm, located just outside a small farming community forty miles north of Nashville, Tennessee. Here he would grow into a fine young man, and here he would leave this world for the next. But wait! We're getting of ourselves!

Many of the details regarding exactly when and how the land came into the possession of Jacob Williams (Ed's great-great-grandfather), who had migrated to the United States from Ireland some one hundred years before, was somewhat obscure. He evidently had come to this country with a large amount of money, supposedly from the sale of his family's estate in Dublin. He settled in this area north of Nashville. Recently declared the capital of Tennessee, Nashville had quickly offered a lot of business opportunities throughout the area. One of the most promising was cotton farming and timber. Jacob quickly began buying up small farms around the area where the family farm was now located. His plan was to combine them into one large enterprise. He was very successful at that and was soon one of the largest landowners in the area. He built a reputation as an honest businessman, generous to all. That included the local Cherokee Indians. Within a few years of his settling here, he married a Cherokee chieftain's daughter and soon began producing offspring. By the end of the first decade of the 1800s, he had three sons and two daughters. In those days, marrying an Indian brought some serious repercussions. At first, it affected Jacob's dealings around town. The label "squaw man" was often attached to his name. However, family history claimed it was always in private, as Jacob was quick with his temper and his firearm.

According to the history of the area, it was in May of 1838 that the first Cherokee roundup took place. In June, the first group of Cherokee was driven west under federal guard along what would become known as the Trail of Tears. For a while, this move was halted due to the drought, the worst in recorded history and became what was called the "sickly season." Thirteen thousand Cherokee were held in military stockades to wait out the drought; fifteen hundred would die during that time. In August, the stockade chiefs met in council to reaffirm the sovereignty of the Cherokee Nation. Then, in September, the drought broke, and the forced march began again. Ed's great-great-grandmother, who was full-blooded Cherokee, had been forced to join the Trail of Tears and relocated to Oklahoma. The story is that she was never heard from again. Jacob's three sons were reported to have joined an antigovernment group fighting against the government's action toward the Indians. Rumor has it that some of Ed's ancestors on that side of the family had fought along in some of the later Indian uprisings. No one knew for sure.

Ed's great-grandfather had left for the Civil War as a twenty-two-year-old captain in the Confederate Army. Kissing his young wife, heavy with child (Ed's grandfather), good-bye, neither could know that they would never lay eyes on each other in this life again. Only a few months later, Captain Williams would be one of only 731 men of Colonel Munson R. Hill's Tennessee Regiment, that would attempt to provide reinforcement to generals Johnston and Beauregard at the Battle of Shiloh. He would be shot off his horse with the first charge. Ed's great-grandmother would stay there on the farm, raising Ed's grandfather, Ernest Williams. Ernest would become very familiar with the dreams of his father for a military career. As an army colonel, he would become a Rough Rider, charging up San Juan Hill right next to Theodore Roosevelt. He would return to Tennessee and become a member of the Tennessee legislature. But the family farm and his family would always be his first priority. And he had a special love for his oldest grandson: Ed. Ed would grow up strong and straight.

Ed's father, Jesse, had the farm as his life's focus. Many of his forebears had been strong military men. All he wanted to do was turn the farm into a booming enterprise for his family. Under his management, it had become one of the largest in the production of timber and cotton from the Alabama/Tennessee line to the Tennessee/Kentucky line. And he loved mules. He considered them the backbone of not only the timber industry but of all types of farming. He became one of the largest mule traders in the area. One of his pet peeves was to see the automobile (in his mind, a device of questionable value) begin to push out the trusty mule as the prime mode of transportation. He felt there would never be a gasoline engine that could out-power a good pair of Kentucky blacks. He had built a huge barn and mule yard just to the north of the main house. At any given time, you would see at least four hundred mules there. Jesse (or Jake, as he was called) was known as the king of all mule breakers.

Now, there are several different ways of breaking a mule to either ride or work. There was another mule dealer, who lived about twenty miles down the road. He was known for his abuse of mules, having killed several in the process. One of the hands, skilled at riding, would mount the mule that was in need of breaking. There would be nothing but a large rope tied around the animal's withers. The mule would be blindfolded, and his back feet would be shackled. Once the breaker had mounted the mule, the blindfold would be removed and the feet unshackled. Another man on another mule would begin to whip the mule being broken with a bullwhip. Of course, the mule would begin to jump and kick. The beating would continue until the mule being broken was too weak to stand up, much less buck any more. Jesse hated that, and despite his Christian attempts, he hated any so-called mule breaker who would treat his mules that way. Ed remembered one conversation between his dad and granddad. It was at the end of winter and time to begin breaking a new crop of mules for the sale in Nashville. As usual, the family had finished supper and was sitting in the living room around the fireplace, still needed on most nights. Jesse was trying to buy out the mule dealer down the road. So far, there had been no agreement. Jesse hated to see another season of abuse take place. He and Grandpa were sitting in their straight-back chairs, staring into the fire. Jesse spoke. "Dad, every time I think about all the torture that goes on at the Wilkins's place, I get so mad I could just walk up and knock him in the dirt and then open the gate and let all his mules out. Why can't he see that there is no need for all the brutality he uses to break mules?"

"Jesse, it's not just Bret. His old man was that way. In fact, so was his granddad. He comes by his meanness honestly."

Jesse continued. "If he could just see that the best way to break a mule is with gentleness and a soft touch. Sure, they are basically mean and like to kick the stuffin' out of you. But they will respond to kindness." Both stopped talking for a bit, staring into the fire.

The old man spoke first. "Jess, it's that way with folks. No matter how mean they are, with enough kindness and soft words, they will usually give kindness and soft words back." Those words would be implanted in Ed's heart for many years to come. Before the breaking season really got started, a mule kicked and killed Bret Wilkins. His widow was more than glad to make a deal with Jesse for the mule business.

As already mentioned, a large part of the Williams farm operation was timber. The family had always dealt somewhat in timber but on a much smaller basis. Jesse had been able to buy up several smaller parcels of raw timber, greatly enlarging his timber holdings. Now, with over nine thousand acres of raw timber, sawmills from as far away as the Northeast had started to approach Jesse about buying timber. There was often one interfering factor. The largest timber operations in the country were generally located near major waterways, where the logs could be floated downstream to the mills. That was not the case here. Logs would be hauled on huge logging trailers, pulled by double teams of mules to the Nashville sawmill. After being cut into boards, they would be taken by train to their destinations around the country. Each year, Jesse would pick out a particular spot where the saw timber was getting heavy. He would sell the trees to the highest bidder, so each year the timber business would grow larger.

This business soon made the Williams Timber Company the largest around. That meant Jesse would need to buy more equipment, such items as skidding harnesses for the mules and several huge trailers designed to carry massive loads of logs to the sawmill. One of the timber companies Jesse started doing business with began trying to convince him to get at least one truck to use in his operation. They even offered to partner with him in the huge cost for such equipment. Jesse resisted, believing that such equipment would never take the place of mules. But finally he succumbed, buying a well-worn Kelly-Springfield (K-S) logging truck with a three-speed transmission and rated at three tons. Jesse made it a point to prove that a team of mules would always be better. But progress would have its way, and by the time Ed finished high school, there would be more trucks and gas-powered skidders in the woods than mules. Ed was a lot more excited at the prospect of driving one of those monster trucks than working behind a team of mules.

But his dad had other plans for him. There had been too many good men maimed or killed in the logging woods. He would not allow Ed to put his life in such danger. He just felt that the Lord had other plans for his eldest son. Oh he had his responsibilities, for sure. By the time he was a senior in school, he was working as field boss in the cotton fields. This involved supervising the weighing of the cotton and paying over two hundred hands. But he always had one eye on the logging operation. There were memories that just would not leave his mind.

When this addition to the family business first really started to grow, Ed was about twelve years old. Because of the danger involved in logging, Ed and his brothers were never allowed to get very close to what was happening. They could stand across the road, where they could generally look across and see the action taking place. Ed can still remember the hugeness of it all. The teams of gigantic Kentucky black mules hooked up to logs that often were six feet across, and fifty feet long. The mules would come out of the woods at nearly a dead run, the log trying to catch up with them. And standing on the log would be either his dad or one of the many hands hired for this operation. The mules would pull the log up to what was called a landing. This was an area slightly elevated above the road. The log trailer would be parked on the road, down below the landing. The long log would be "bucked" into shorter lengths. Hooked to the trailer would sometimes be six to eight mules. Each log would be rolled down the slight incline of the landing, with as many as ten hands using cant hooks. Once started, the log would be rolled onto the trailer. Nearly every season there would be at least one worker who would be either hurt or killed. It was the nature of the work.

Life was good in those days. There was always activity on the farm. Jesse and Janie were very active in the small Baptist church in town. The church wasn't large enough to support a full-time pastor, so Brother Malcolm worked part time on the Williams's farm. He was really good with equipment and was in charge of keeping such things as plows, wagons, and as the inventory of gasoline-powered devices increased, all repaired and in good working order.

At least once every month during the summer, Jesse would hold a youth campout down at the old pond. If you stood on the north end of the porch, behind the swing, and looked at about a 45-degree angle to the house, you could see the pond glistening in the sun. It covered about five acres, was bordered by trees on three sides, and had a nice beach on the house side.

There was this one youth camp that Jesse and the pastor organized in June of 1933, when Ed was ten years old. The kids had started to arrive on Friday evening, about five o'clock. The plans were for a wiener roast about dark, some singing around a campfire, and then a message by Brother Malcolm. This wasn't Ed's first youth campout. But things were different this year. Before, he had listened to the message, but only "sort of." This year, when Brother Malcolm began to explain what Jesus had done and how a person could secure his place in His family, something happened deep inside. After the plan of salvation was explained, Brother Malcolm asked each kid to find a place away from the campfire where they could be alone. There they were challenged to just talk to God about their life and do whatever they felt He was telling them to do. Ed had sat next to an old stump that had been there, according to his grandfather, since his great-grandfather was a kid. It felt and looked almost like it was petrified. There he began to talk to God as only a child can. "God," he started, "I really don't know what to say. I think I believe that Jesus died on a cross so He could forgive my sins. But I don't really know of any sins I have committed. I have been in a couple of fights at school. There were two or three times when I was late getting home from school because I stopped by a friend's house, but I told Mom I had stayed at school to help the teacher clean up the classroom. I guess that was lying. I guess all I can say is that I want to live my life for you, and I want to go to heaven when I die. So, Jesus, forgive me of my sins, and come into my heart and save me." That was it! But the feeling was overwhelming. And that feeling lasted for years. As Ed went through his teen years, there were times when it would seem to descend below the surface. But it was always there, waiting to be brought up at the right time. Because of that event, the pond and the old stump would hold lifelong memories for Ed.

There was another site that was special. This was the huge old cottonwood tree that stood about thirty feet in front of the porch. He and his two brothers would play every hero they had ever read about while circling that tree. During the course of their growing up, they had become acquainted with every limb that hung from the old tree. Ed knew it was old, because he had heard his dad tell stories about playing at the base of the tree when he was a small boy.

Close to his heart was the house where he would spend his entire life. It was very typical for that part of the country. It was actually two houses, tied together with what was called a dog trot. This was an open area about 30 feet wide, and the same depth as the house. It had a cover, much like the rest of the roof on the house. The floor was wood planks, again, much like the floors inside the main part of the house. This open area served to tie together the bedrooms, located in this case on the right side of the dog trot, from the kitchen and living room, located on the left side. There was no indoor water or plumbing of any kind until about two years before Ed graduated high school. But neither was there in any of the other farmhouses in the area. During cold months, the family would sleep in the bedrooms located in that area to the right side of the dog trot. The beds, covers, and pillows were all filled with feathers. If you needed to use the bathroom at night, there was a rather large bucket that sat at the foot of the bed for that purpose. If you didn't want to use that ... well, the little building designed for that purpose was just off the end of the dog trot and about thirty yards down a path. Very few of the family members ever chose that during the winter months. And even during the summer months, one might meet a visitor during the trip. It could be anything from a skunk to a bobcat. In the winter, as soon as it began to get light, one by one the family member would grab their clothes and dash across the dog trot and into the living room and to the roaring fireplace. The womenfolk would already be cooking biscuits, bacon, hotcakes, and scrambled eggs. Fresh milk and hot coffee was always available.

Ed Finds the Love of His Life

Irma considered herself a natural matchmaker. She had already paired up three couples from church. Only one had been successful, but that was good enough for Irma. She was Jesse Williams's second cousin. That made her family. Her husband, Blake, had a niece (whose name was Susan) that Irma just knew deep down inside was specially designed for Jesse eldest son, Ed. She was fourteen, just one year younger than Ed. It was a natural match. And Irma had a plan. She was known far and wide for her cooking. Few church members would turn down a Sunday invitation to dinner after the morning service. So that was the plan. She would invite Ed to come to her house for Sunday dinner. She would invite Susan to her house on Saturday. Susan would spend the night and go to church with them on Sunday. It was a divine plan that was sure to work. But there was a problem. Susan's dad, Jake, was super-protective of Susan. In his mind, any boy interested in Susan was up to no good. Maybe it was based on his own youth. Who knows? But he had already proclaimed that there was not a boy in the area who was good enough for his Susan. They had not lived in the area but about two years, but that proclamation had been sounded before they even got unpacked. So Irma would need to be very cunning if she was going to pull off this matchup. There was no way she could make this plan work if Jake had any idea what was going on. But he just might let Susan come over to her house on Saturday to spend the night. With that in mind, she hooked up her buggy on Friday afternoon and headed off to Jake and Lillian's house.

Pulling the horse up short just in front of the Haskins's house, she stepped out of the buggy and threw a half hitch around the hitching post. Her horse had been known to wander if not secured. Not only that, but Jake had recently bought something called a "pickup truck," and it was nowhere to be seen. That meant he was out in the contraption somewhere. If her horse wasn't secure and Jake came home in that thing, she would be walking the five miles home. It had seemed strange to her that a man who made his living shoeing horses would stoop so low as to buy a car, or truck, or whatever it was. Oh well!

She mounted the steps to the porch, walked to the front door, and knocked. Susan's mother, Lillian, came to the door, wiping her hands on her apron. She was fixing lunch. As far as cooking goes, she was Irma's closest competitor. "Hey Lillian," she started the conversation.

"Has Susan got home from school yet?" Irma quizzed.

"Why no," Lillian answered. "Why would she be home this early? It's not even noon yet!"

Irma felt stupid. This just wasn't going as planned. "Well, the church is having a special youth service this Sunday, and I wondered if Susan could come to my house on Saturday, spend the night, and go to church with us Sunday morning? We'll bring her home Sunday afternoon."

"Well," Lillian slowly answered, looking at some point on the porch floor, "I'll have to check with Jake before I can answer. You know how he is about Susan."

"Yeh, I know," responded Irma. "Jake can be a real jerk." Lillian's eyes flashed at Irma, but for only a second. She knew how he was, but she didn't like anyone reminding her.

They heard the roar in the distance, heading toward the house. Both knew it to be Jake's old truck. He was heading for home, kicking up clouds of dust that was visible from two miles away. That was good. Irma would just wait. He didn't intimate her.

Jake and his Model T truck came sliding through the dirt up to the house. Irma's horse jerked on the rein securing him. She hoped he didn't break it. He would be gone, sure enough, if that happened. Jake killed the motor and stepped out onto the running board. Being rather short, standing on the running board made him able to look down on those around him. Irma glared at him for scaring her horse. "Need to get with the times, old girl," he shot (in good humor). "This is the transportation of the future."

Irma sort of snorted in the direction of the car. "Only for people with no brains, as far as I can see," she retorted.

Lillian quickly explained why Irma was there. Before she even completed her request, Jake snapped back a hasty, "No! I don't trust you," he said, looking at Irma. "You'll have her married off before she can even cook."

This made Irma mad. "Why are so intent on making that girl's life miserable. She is going to spread her wings regardless of what you say. She will do it under your direction or on her own. It's a force of nature that you can't control."

For what seemed like too long, they just starred at each other. Jake was the first to speak. "Okay," he said. "Just make sure you keep an eye on her. In fact, we just might come to church Sunday morning so I can keep an eye on you."

That, Irma had not expected. He being there would foul up everything. Her mind responded quickly. "Oh Jake, the service is just for kids. You really wouldn't like it."

Jake grunted and stomped into the house. Lillian smiled at Irma. "Should she walk to your house, or do you want to pick her up?"

"I will pick her up tomorrow, about three in the afternoon."

"Sounds good!" With that, Irma untied her horse, climbed aboard the buggy, and trotted on down the road, smiling all the way.

Jesse and the Williams family arrived early to church, as usual. Jesse helped set up things for the Sunday service. It was late November, and the old pot-bellied stove had to be lit in time for the sanctuary to be heated before members started to arrive. Ed would usually help set out the songbooks, making sure that there was one for each two seats. Then, as soon as some of the other guys begin to arrive, they would find a place where they could talk about school activities and girls. Girls mostly! Today, because it was cold, the guys had decided to sit about midway in the sanctuary. Ed's back was to the door. As people began to arrive, he would turn to see who had come in. His mother had told him that Irma was bringing a guest with her. Supposedly, it was one of her kinfolk … a girl about his age … to meet him. He had seen some of her attempts at matchmaking, and he had not been impressed.

Ed heard the door open. He turned slightly, so he could look over his shoulder. He froze! Entering through the door in front of Irma and her husband, Blake, was the most beautiful female he had ever seen. She was tall, with coal-black hair that hung over her shoulders. She had on a blue, flowered, full dress. But it was her eyes that held him spellbound. They were the color of nothing he had ever seen: a dark blue with sort of a sparkle. At least, that is what he thought as he looked at them. His own eyes were about to pop, or at least that's the way they felt. She gave him sort of a side glance and then looked back at Irma for directions as to where to sit. Irma, of course, directed her to the seat beside Ed. She chose, instead, to sit on the other side of the aisle, but Ed was hooked! In that moment, he knew he would never be interested in another girl in his entire life. It seemed obvious that she had no interest in him, but at the moment, that did not matter.

Determined not to allow her plan to be foiled, Irma sat beside Ed. Her husband stood in the aisle, as Irma motioned for Susan to take the seat beside her. Ed dared not look to see how she responded to this demand. Through his side vision, however, he was aware of her crossing the aisle and sitting beside Irma. Blake then slid into the seat beside her. Irma sort of leaned back in her seat, leaving room for the two youngsters to be in full view of each other. "Susan, meet Ed. Ed, meet Susan. You two will be eating dinner at my house today, so you might as well be friendly." That was sure okay by Ed. He wasn't too sure about Susan.

All during the service, Ed wanted to look over at her to see if, by any remote chance, she might be looking at him. But he didn't dare. So much of this feeling was new to him. There had been a few local girls he had liked, but not like this. He had been told that Susan and her family had only recently moved here from Birmingham, Alabama. Blake, Irma's husband and Jakes cousin, had helped him get a job shoeing horses at a local horse farm. That was his profession, and he was one of the best in that part of the country. Jake had been able to rent a small place that was owned by the horse farm. Although it was fairly close to the William's farm, it was just across the county line. That put Susan in a different high school. That's why, even though they lived fairly close, he had never seen her. As the service progressed thorough the singing, and as Brother Malcolm began to preach, all sorts of questions raced through Ed's mind. Did she have a boyfriend? Was she stuck up? With looks like that, she must be.

As soon as service was over, Susan and Irma headed out the door, followed dutifully by Blake. He disliked these matchmaking affairs, but he knew better than to try and stop Irma once she had her hat fixed. Irma had never been able to have children, and Blake figured trying to bring together young couples was the best alternative to having her own. This matchup seemed to be her crowning achievement. Having Susan over seemed to have lit a fire in Irma that Blake had missed. And having Jesse Williams and his family over for Sunday dinner was a joy beyond words. All this could not have made life any better this sunshiny Sunday morning.

Ed quickly caught up with them, hoping he might get the chance to at least help Susan up into the buggy. After all, that was just the gentlemanly thing to do. Surely, she would not refuse him that, even if she did not particularly like him. He was almost overwhelmed when she extended her hand for him to help her up and into the tiny backseat. Irma and her husband occupied the front seat.

What Ed had really hoped for was the chance to invite Susan to ride out to Irma's house in his family's brand new motorcar. Jesse had recently condescended to buying a 1936 Ford, four-door sedan. The timber business had been especially good that year, and he had decided to splurge on something never before splurged on by the Williams family. Ed had been practicing out behind the barn and was getting pretty good at driving. But the opportunity for the invite did not present itself, so Ed was content with holding her hand for the few seconds it took for her to step up into the buggy.

Irma looked around Susan, who had quickly seated herself in the backseat. She looked first of all at Ed and then at his hand, still firmly holding Susan's, although she was already seated. Irma smiled and then spoke. "Well, are you going to trot alongside us all the way, holding her hand, or do you want to act like you have the good sense you were born with and climb up on the seat?" That question required no answer. Susan scooted to the other side of the seat, and Ed quickly sat down beside her. She looked down at their hands, and sort of shook hers loose from his rather tight grip.

Ed glanced down at his dad in the shiny, black Ford that he pulled up fairly close to the buggy. Not close enough to spook Irma's horse, that was slowly getting used to the noisy things, but close enough to grin at Ed. "Go ahead," he shouted. "Guess I know what's important! I was going to let you drive. But I guess that's out. See you guys at Irma's!" And off he went, kicking up dust from the back tires.

After a fabulous meal, everyone moved into the living room. It was still pretty cold outside, so Irma had asked Blake if he would build a fire. He had already started the process, but Irma was like that … always telling folks what to do before it was necessary. Now, with the roaring fire going, it was about to get too hot in the house. Ed stood up, stretching as he moved toward the front door. He walked out on the porch and leaned against one of the posts holding up the porch roof. He gazed out across the field to the woods on the far side. He was in love! He couldn't understand it, since he had known Susan for less than a day. But he just knew it! She had been in the kitchen, helping Irma and his mom clean up. He had noticed his mom several times, as she glanced at him and then at Susan. Ed could only hope that she was thinking what a great daughter-in-law Susan would make and not considering how she would stop this match before it went too far. She was very aware of Irma's matchmaking attempts and had often commented how she should mind her own business. There were a number of folks around these parts who felt the same way, and some had expressed such. But that didn't faze Irma. She was convinced that this was her God-given calling.

Ed heard the front door open and close behind him. He half turned to see who was coming outside on this rather blustery day. Much to his surprise—and thrill—it was Susan. She walked over to the porch swing and sat down. The cool breeze caused her to shiver. She crossed her arms, pulling her sweater up around her. The old springs holding the swing to the eyebolts creaked as she started a slow swing. He turned to look at her. "Get plenty to eat?" he asked. Suddenly, that sounded so stupid.

"Sure did!" she answered.

The conversation continued. "Have you been out here to Irma's much?"

"Only twice. We haven't been here long. We moved up here from Birmingham so Daddy could get a better job. Funny he would have to come way out here in the sticks to get a better job than he had in the city."

"What does he do?" asked Ed.

"He's a horseshoe specialist." She sort of laughed as she answered.

"He's what?" Ed asked.

"Well, he can design special shoes for horses that have trouble walking right. There is a huge horse ranch near where we live, and the owners hired Daddy to do all the foot work on their racehorses. I'm sure you have heard of it. Russell Hills Farm? The pay is really good, and Daddy was able to get us a real neat place. And he bought a pickup truck for his tools. It's used and noisy, but I guess it runs good. Things are really going good. It's just that …" she hesitated. "He's so strict on me. He treats me like a baby. Why, if he knew I was here, on this porch, with you … alone," her voice sort of drifted off, "he would just have a tizzy."

Ed moved toward the swing. Susan was sitting in the middle. She moved to the edge, inviting him to sit down. His heart skipped at least a hundred beats … or so it seemed. "You know, I don't blame your dad for trying to protect you. You are absolutely beautiful." Ed swallowed hard, not believing what he had just said. She didn't slap him, so he assumed all was okay. She blushed a deep crimson and thanked him.

Susan was one year behind Ed in school. When they met, Ed was in the tenth grade; Susan was in the ninth. The fact they did not go to the same school was torture for them both. That meant they could only see each other on weekends, and not every weekend. However, some six months after they met, Irma could not stand it anymore. On one find spring afternoon, she arrived at the Haskins's house at about the same time as Jake arrived home. She and Blake had bought a 1929 Model T roadster. So, she roared up at about the same time he did. Both were like teenagers. He had always been a bit immature, but this truck seemed to have driven him backward. As Jake dismounted his truck, he cast a smirk at Irma's little car. "Some people never grow up," he said in her direction. Without saying anything further, he went off to the barn to feed his three pigs. It was about thirty minutes before he returned to the house. Irma was not going to go away if she had to sit in the swing 'til morning. He smiled as he mounted the top porch step. Irma and Lillian were sitting in swing. "What brings you way out here, old girl? Trying to show me up in your hot rod? Want to race?"

Irma refused to grace that question with an answer. He had called her "old girl" for as long as she could remember. "Your daughter," she snapped.

That brought Jake up short on his path through the front door. "What do you mean?"

"Sit down, and listen to me!"

Wiping his hands on the front of his Levis, he sat down in a chair facing the swing. "Talk, woman," he snapped.

"Have you noticed your daughter lately?"

"What a dumb question! What do you mean? Is something wrong?"

"There sure is. She's growing up, and you still see her as a baby."

"She is a baby ... my baby!"

"You gonna keep her that way all her life?"

"Well no. There'll come a time for her to grow up. Just not yet."

"You blind fool! She's growing up right under your eyes, and you're missing some of the most important times of her life."

"What do you mean?"

"What I mean is ..." Irma decided she might as well blurt it out. "She's in love."

Jake shot straight up out of the chair. "With who?"

"I won't say until you calm down and agree to listen."

He shot a stormy glance at Lillian. "Did you know anything about this?"

"I'm as in the dark as you are!" Jake sat back down.

Irma continued. "His name is Ed Williams," she began. "His family owns the large farm and lumber operation you might know as Williams Timber Company."

Jake's jaw dropped. "You mean Jesse Williams's oldest boy?"

Yep, that's him."

"Why, Jesse Williams is one of the finest men I have ever met. In fact, I was just over to his place, looking at some horses he wants me to shoe. I saw a young man over there who seemed to be in charge of the farm. In fact, Jesse introduced me to him. Seemed like a really nice young man." He gazed at nothing in particular. "When did this all happen?" Irma started to explain, but Jake interrupted. "Don't tell me! Just answer. Was this another one of your matchmaking projects?"

"Jake, I cannot tell a lie. If ever in my life I have seen two young people who were meant for each other, it's these two."

Jake stood to his full height. "Okay! I want that boy over here this Saturday for supper. I will size him up, and if I figger he is worthy of my Susan ... well ... then we'll see." And that was that. He was off into the house, yelling for Lillian to feed him his supper. It was only then that Irma noticed a beautiful and excited face peering between parted curtains in what Irma knew was Susan's bedroom. She had heard every word.

During the next eighteen months, the love between Susan and Ed grew. They often talked about the future. But the future held the possibility of dark clouds. There was a lot of talk about the rumblings of war in Europe. If the United States got fully involved in the war, Ed, along with many other young men, may have their life's plans interrupted. Ed's family had long been involved in the defense of their country. Jesse was the only male Williams who had not been in the military in recent family history. That was primarily due to the fact that, during his youth, there was no national conflict that made it necessary to join up. In addition, the growing timber business provided a service to the nation that was, in the minds of many, more necessary than Jesse letting the farm go in order to spend a few years as a soldier. But that might not be the case for Ed. Time would be the dictator of his actions.

Then, on December 7, 1941, it happened: the Japanese bombed Pearl Harbor in Hawaii. War in Europe involving the Germans had begun in 1939. Until Pearl Harbor, the United States had not been directly involved in the conflict. But after the attack by the Japanese and the declaration of war with Japan, the United States was sort of forced into the conflict in Europe. There was now a national rush to man the American army and protect our nation. As Ed and Susan, as well as their parents, listened to the radio and read the accounts in the newspapers, it soon became obvious what Ed must do.

It was early summer of 1942 when Ed decided he would enlist in the army. When he told his dad, Jesse was, of course, proud. The only thing Jesse would have liked for Ed to do was go to officer training school. Even though Jesse had never been in the military, his grandfather and great-grandfather had all been officers in the army. For Ed to go in as an enlisted man was not exactly what Jesse wanted for his son. But Ed would have it no other way. He had no intention of making a career out of it. All he wanted to do was help defend his homeland and then come home.

It would be about thirty days before Ed would leave, and there was much to do. For one thing, there was Susan. She was the love of his life. Although they had known each other for only a couple of years, it was as though they had been in love all their short lives. They had spent countless hours talking about their future together. Even though there had been nothing official, it was an accepted fact between the two of them that their lives would be spent together. Ed wanted to make things more official before he left. But as he pondered that, he began to have second thoughts. What if he didn't come back? Would it be right to put Susan through that? Would it be better to sort of hold off on everything until he got back after the war? They talked. Susan wasn't in full agreement with that idea. However, she did see the wisdom of waiting on any sort of commitment or engagement. Both knew that if it were God's will that they be together, the waiting would be okay. One night just before he was due to depart, they had one final discussion on the matter. It took place while sitting at the foot of the old stump on the Williams family farm. That stump had been a silent listener to so many vital and important events in this family. Several of the Williams's ancestors, as well as Ed himself, had met with God at the base of this historic site. It was only fitting that Ed and Susan settle on some of their plans here.

They had been sitting on the small sandy area between the stump and the water's edge. They had sat silently, leaning against the stump, for several minutes. Every so often, Ed would pick up a stone and toss it into the pond, and watch as the ripples spread out. "Those ripples look sort of like our future right now," Ed mused. "We just don't know exactly where it will all end. Sort of like we can't tell where the ripples will end."

After a long pause, Susan spoke. "Ed, you know that I love you with all my heart, don't you?"

"Sure," Ed answered. "And I feel the same about you. I cannot imagine going through life without us being together. It just all seems right!"

"It is right!" answered Susan. "But now we are at a crossroads … all because of this stupid war. And our lives will never be the same. What do you suggest we do?"

That was something Ed did not want to get into, but he knew they must. He had lain awake at night, turning all the options over in his mind. He had even toyed with both of them running away, hiding out in some remote place until all this was over. Yet, Ed knew that was not who he and Susan were. They would be forced to face the time apart and depend on God to bring them back together. His next words were formed slowly and deliberately. "Susan, I do not believe we need to make any really tight plans about the future. We both know that it is within the realm of possibility that I might not return from the war."

Susan tried to stifle a sob, but it came out anyway. "I know that is a reality, but I have refused to allow myself to even think about that," she sobbed. "I must place my trust in God that He will bring you back to me!" Suddenly, Ed turned toward her, taking her in his arms. They wept together. And this would be the last of such talk. For the remaining days, they enjoyed each other and the other family members. There were a number of things planned by the community, not only for Ed, but for several other young men who would be leaving at the same time. From now on, nothing but positive attitudes.

All too soon, the time of Ed's departure arrived. All his life he was to remember that farewell. Saying goodbye to his family was hard. But leaving Susan...... that was the hardest. As he hugged each one, little did he know it would be the last time he would see his dad this side of eternity. As he looked into Jesse's strong Native American eyes, he realized just how much he owed this man. His dad locked eyes with him, and he spoke. "Ed," he said, "always remember who you are and who you belong to." Those words would be remembered many times before Ed returned to this spot.

Good-byes said, Ed climbed aboard the old bus for Nashville and then onto the train for basic camp. Every emotion in him screamed for him to get off the bus and head for the woods. But he knew such an act would ruin his life. So, being the man he would become, he seated himself and looked out the window for as long as he could see his family and Susan waving good-bye.

Shortly after completing basic training, Ed got his shipping orders. In about thirty days, he would board a troop ship for overseas. Judging from Ed's life, one would assume he would head for Tennessee, his family, and Susan by the quickest means possible. But life in basic training had begun to change Ed in ways he did not like. Before camp, his life had been extremely sheltered. He had never gotten drunk, been with a woman, or been in a fight. Now, by going off the base with some of the guys he had met in basic training, he had tasted the sweet wine of sin. The possibility of not returning from the war was always on his mind, so he figured, why not? And it would most likely be the same for any young man leaving for who knows what. Ed had decided he owed it to himself to get some experiences he may never have the chance to get again.

He decided that instead of going home, he would spend the thirty days with his buddies. But this had not worked out exactly as he had expected. As the time drew near for him to leave, the guilt about not going home grew from a gnawing aggravation to a flood of pain. Now he couldn't even bring himself to call his folks. His dad has installed the first phone in the community in the dog trot, so all the neighbors could have access to it. It would be no problem to call and talk to the entire family. But he just could not face trying to justify why he had chosen to stay at camp rather than see his folks one last time. And Susan? The guilt of some of the things he had done in the past few months would not allow him to even say hello to her. He was miserable. But at last, it was time to go, and he was able to shove it all to the back of his mind.

Ed and several hundred other young troops rode the train from Ft. Benning, Georgia, to New York. There, they boarded the troop ship *Strathaird* on January 15, 1943. They were heading for Belfast, North Ireland, where they were scheduled to arrive on January 26. Of the hundreds on board, all but a few were miserable with seasickness. For whatever reason, Ed didn't seem to be bothered all that much. One of the guys he had gotten acquainted with during basic was named Tim. He seemed to be suffering more than most of the others. He spent the majority of the time draped over the fan tail, gagging and cursing.

After several days of this, the sea grew somewhat calm. As the huge ship settled into the swells, many of the men began to recover slightly. Tim was even able to sit on top of the battle tanks lashed down on the deck and talk. Ed had spent quite a bit of time straddling the barrel of one of the cannons. One day, Tim crawled up on the one next to Ed's. "Tell me Ed," he said, "what is it with you? How come you are always so laid-back? The rest of these jerks are scared, including me. But you! You just seem to be so cool. Well, except for a couple of times when you lost it. Why is that?"

Ed thought for a moment before answering. A few months ago, he would have given Tim an answer that may have really provided food for thought and done so without thinking. But now? He had done and said things he never would have believed. He knew Tim had seen and heard him on several occasions. He formed his words carefully. "Tim," he started, "please don't look at me as any sort of example. In these last weeks, I have not really been what I was raised to be. But regardless of my weaknesses, I

tian. I am scared and lonely. I get mad and then I get disgusted.
dless of that, I am still a believer in Jesus Christ.

h," replied Tim, "I've heard that crap before. Thanks for nothin'."
He slid down off the tank and meandered over to a group of guys shooting craps. *Well, I sure have blown my testimony,* Ed thought.

The first few weeks were sort of boring. Most days, Ed and his squad would go out on reconnaissance missions. They spent most of their recon time sneaking around in the cold mud and slop, looking for any kind of enemy activity. When they spotted movement, they would radio the position and other information to headquarters. Then they would hunker down in a hole or ditch, while the big guns dropped shells on them. Occasionally, a squadron of airplanes would dive out of the sky, flying just above the ground, and drop explosives on the enemy. During those times, Ed would wonder just what he was doing there. With a bit of different planning, he could have been flying one of those.

On one particular mission, they were ordered to go deeper into enemy territory than they had before. There was a lot of apprehension among the men. There had been reports of some huge enemy troop buildups, and the CO wanted some proof by visual recon, not just rumor. The squad dispatched for this assignment consisted of one lieutenant, one sergeant, and six grunts; Ed and Tim were among the grunts. It was just after sunup, and there was a heavy fog lying right on the ground. All was quiet as they crept along. They had traveled about six miles when it seemed as though Germans suddenly came out of the ground. They were surrounded. It happened so fast, until there was no gunfire; there was only yelling for the Americans to drop their weapons. It was obvious that to resist would be useless, so all eight Americans complied. They were quickly searched, bound together with ropes, and marched off through the fog. It took about ten hours of forced march to finally arrive at the small railroad site, where the locomotive with the huge swastika painted on the front and sides sat, chugging and belching plumbs of white steam. Tied to its tail was a string of cattle cars. The Americans were quickly shoved into the filthy cars and ordered to sit on the floor. It was several more hours before the train finally moved. During that time, they noticed the arrival of several more groups, not all of them were Americans. By peering through the boarded sides of their car, they could see that many of the new arrivals had some sort of insignia, like a star, painted on their clothes. They were not dressed like soldiers, but like civilians. And they seemed to be treated much rougher than they had been.

During all this time, there was no water or food offered. There were about twenty other Americans in the same car with Ed and Tim, and they were all equally terrified. They occasionally whispered to each other about what might happen next. They had all heard stories about how the Germans would sometimes stop at some lonely place, unload the prisoners, and execute them on the spot. Some were praying, and some were cursing the entire situation. Ed was praying; Tim was cursing.

They rode on the smelly train for about a week. There had been no bathroom facilities and very little food and water. They were only allowed to get out of the cars once each day. If anybody was caught sitting down or walking too far from the others, he was slammed to the ground and beaten with batons.

Finally, the train pulled up alongside what they soon learned would be their home for the next two years, though there would be none of the comforts of home or even of basic training. Several of the guys had dysentery by the time they arrived. Most of those would die within the first few days of arrival.

After several weeks, things sort of settled in. A number of those who had originally arrived at the camp with Ed had died—in addition to the ones who were sick when they arrived. The trip had just been too rough on them. Life was really tough. These Germans were not nice people.

The weeks, the months, and the first year flew by as though a dream. Ed wanted all this hell to be pushed as far into deepest recesses of his mind as possible. As time slipped by, so did the original hope that they would be rescued quickly. Winter came, with its bitter cold, constant snow, and ice. This gave way to what seemed to be unending rain and mud. Then came summer, with its high humidity and searing heat.

Morale was always very low. This gave way to fights and, on some occasions, murders between the POWs. Ed tried as best he could to remember what his life was like before. He tried to pray. On one occasion, one of the Christian guards smuggled in about a dozen Bibles. Several of the guys used the pages as rolling papers for cigarettes. But others, including Ed, found a real source of strength and hope in the pages. One of the guys, who had been a minister before joining, started a Bible study. It was in one of those that Ed finally found his way back to his faith. After that, he felt he could do what needed to be done when he got home—if he ever did.

After about two years, they were liberated. It happened on a bright, sunshiny day in July. They woke up to what sounded like heavy gunfire, which seemed to be about five or so miles away. As it moved closer, the prisoners could see the German guards, hauling stuff out of the headquarters shack and loading it onto trucks. Suddenly, all the trucks sped off, and there was silence. The camp was deserted, except for the prisoners. They had been warned that if the Allies ever made an attempt to liberate them they would all be shot before it could happen. But not one had been shot so far. In fact, the cowards had all turned tail and ran as soon as they found out who was heading their way. Then it happened! From out of the tree line surrounding the camp burst what looked like hundreds of green-clad angels. It turned out to be only about twenty, but that was enough to send the krauts scampering away. It was a wonderful day. Soon, 6 × 6 troop trucks arrived with fresh clothes and C rations. How they had once griped about the GI prepackaged food. Now it would rival the best food in the best restaurant at home. Then, they were loaded up and taken to a MASH unit for medical attention. All Ed could think about was getting home. He could only hope Susan had waited for him. But he knew that it was highly possible she had married. That thought he could barely stand.

There was a shortwave radio at the MASH unit. Using that, the operator could patch into a telephone in the States. It took Ed some time to rummage through what few items he was able to keep while in the POW camp. He knew he had written down the number of the phone his dad had mounted on the dog trot, but it was nowhere to be found. He was frantic! He had to get in touch with his folks.

There were several chaplains at the hospital. All the former prisoners were encouraged to spend at least one session with one of them. The one Ed was sent to was from, or all places, Nashville. When Ed told him of his dilemma, the chaplain had the radio operator place a call to a friend who pastored a church just twenty miles from where Ed lived. Ed knew that God was on the move on his behalf. Within two days, he had the phone number and was told that his folks had been notified he was alive and would be coming home. But not all the news was good. The chaplain's friend had gone to visit Ed's parents, to let them know the news firsthand. Ed's mother had told the pastor that Jesse, Ed's father, had been killed in a tractor accident the year before. Ed's heart broke, as he remembered how he had wasted the last chance to see his dad. That would be a hard one to get victory over. There was no word about Susan, but that did not surprise Ed.

It took Ed several weeks to get home. When he arrived, and his mother gave Ed the details about his dad, the hurt was even deeper than when he first heard the news. After the accident, Jesse had hung on as long as possible, hoping to get some word about Ed. Finally, the injuries, which were severe, took their toll. After his mother completed the story, Ed stumbled out to the old stump. Right now, that was his only point of comfort. He literally hugged the tree and wept from the bottom of his very being. He had missed his last chance to tell his dad how much he meant to him; he chose to party instead. How could he ever look at himself in the mirror again?

Sure enough, Susan was true to her word and had waited for him. But there was one more situation that began to haunt Ed. When he first realized that Susan had waited, he was elated beyond words. It was a few days later, after he was suddenly awakened from a dead sleep, that the full horror of his actions before leaving for the war came crashing in on him. A dark and disturbing question took over his mind. Should he confess all to Susan? If he did, would she forgive him or dump him in disgust? If he didn't tell her, how would that dark secret affect their future lives together? Needless to say, Ed was through with sleep that night—and for several nights later. His days were filled with the dread of approaching this problem in the only real way he could see: coming clean with her and depending on God to soften her heart and allow her to forgive him. He decided to talk to Brother Malcolm. He was still pastor of their small church. He had proven to be a wise counselor. He had helped his mom through his dad's death and helped her stand up under the overwhelming fear her son had perished in the war. Now, Ed desperately needed his help.

Ed sat down in the chair across from Brother Malcolm's small desk in the church office. He had rehearsed what he would say about a thousand times. Yet now, those carefully practiced words just weren't there. Brother

Malcolm finally broke the silence. "Ed, I know you are deeply troubled about something. I've sensed it since you first got back. What is it, boy? There is nothing you have done that He cannot and will not forgive."

"His forgiveness is not the issue" Ed responded. "I cleared that up while I was in the POW camp. It's … Susan's forgiveness I need. And when I tell her what I have done, I cannot see her forgiving me."

"I can imagine what this is about," Brother Malcolm said. "You don't need to go into the details with me. You were a young man, far away from home, about to go into a situation where you very likely would not return."

"Does that make the sin acceptable?" Ed asked.

"Certainly not! You say that you have cleared it with God, and that is the most vital. As long as we are clean before Him, we can face whatever the human results are, even though they may be hard. But you cannot expect to build a life with Susan and still carry this dark secret with you. But I don't believe you need to go into all the details. And she doesn't need to hear the details. I believe just the fact that you are willing to tell her that you did stray from your Christian upbringing and violated her trust in you should set you both free. And incidentally, it's not like you two were already married. That, of course, would make the impact worse. But under the circumstances, if Susan really loves you enough to wait for you, not knowing if you were dead or alive, I surely believe she will weather this little bump in the road of life. Give her a chance to prove her love for you is greater than your sin. However, if you were to decide not to tell her and it somehow came out later in life … well, that might have different results."

Ed didn't feel all that much better as he left Brother Malcolm's office. He decided to walk the seven miles to the church so he could think. Now, he needed more walking time than that just to sort out how he was going to handle this.

He decided to jump right into the situation rather than suffer the torture of putting it off. He felt that each day he delayed would be another day when he felt he was cheating on Susan. He decided to have her meet him at the old stump down by the pond. Once again, this would be a place of reconciliation.

Susan arrived in her little Ford coupe on Saturday afternoon. Ed met her, opened the door of her car, and helped her out. Just being close to her and feeling the overwhelming love he had for her almost made him decide to forgo this idea and take a chance on her never finding out. They began the walk down to the pond. On the way, he reaffirmed there was no choice in the matter. Arriving at the pond edge, they both sat down at the base of the stump. The last time they had sat there was before he left of the war. That conversation was still strong within them both. That is where they had agreed there would be no strings attached to their relationship until—and if—he returned. And now, here they were, and another test was to be taken.

Susan sat quietly, staring into the water. Ed fidgeted with some blades of grass that grew next to where he was sitting. Turning toward her, he opened his mouth to speak. "Susan—"

She gently put her forefinger over his lips, indicating he should not speak. "Ed, I don't pretend to know all that happened while you were gone. I know you have seen some terrible things. Perhaps you have done some terrible things. When I heard you had been captured and were missing, I thought I would die. I wanted to! Then, when I heard you were alive and were coming home to your family—and to me—I struggled with how I would handle some of those things I knew you had gone through. How could I help you through it? I prayed and asked God to allow me to forgive and forget whatever had happened. I believe God brought you back for me ... and for our life together. And I feel He specifically instructed me and then gave me the grace and ability to not only forgive whatever but to have no need to even know the details. Ed, as long as you have received forgiveness from God for whatever happened, that forgiveness counts for me also. In other words, I consider you to be clean and pure before me as you are before God, with no need to tell me anything." Ed broke! He began to weep and embraced this wonderful woman, actually receiving strength from her. God was so good!

They were soon married, and Ed took his place on the family farm and in their timber business. His mother passed away the year after Ed came home. Without her Jesse by her side as her strength, she had lost interest in life.

Ed's brother had bought a hardware store in the small community shortly after his return. He had very little interest in the farm but wanted to start a small hardware chain. And it worked. Within some twelve years, he boasted a chain of eighteen stores, scattered from North Nashville to the Kentucky border.

Life had been good for Ed and his family. He had one son, Rick, of whom he and Susan were very proud. He wanted nothing but to carry on the family farm. He helped Ed enlarge the timber operation even more over the years.

Now, for the rest of our story, let's fast-forward through the years.

Ed is now in his early eighties. Ten years ago, Susan died of cancer after some two years of pain and suffering. Since then, Ed spent most of his time puttering around on the farm. Eight years ago his son, Rick, had totally taken over the operation. Ed was tired and ready to go home. When Susan passed away, that strengthened his resolve not to stick around too much longer. He had suffered a major heart attack, had open-heart surgery, and was in poor health.

Much of the timber operation had been sold off. Mules were only an oddity, no longer used for work. Rick had wanted to delve into the dairy business, so now he had a small herd. He also ran a small herd of Angus cattle, more as a hobby rather than as a cash business. Rick had torn down the old house (caught it just before it fell down) and built a fine, new, four-bedroom, ranch-style house. Nothing would do but for Ed to live out his final years there with them. They had added on a small cottage for him, complete with his own kitchen (although he always ate with the family) and his own entrance. Life was good! The entire family, including Ed, was involved in the small church.

Ed's Last Days

Old Ed sat on the front porch of his son's ranch-style home. The porch ran the entire length of the house, was about twelve feet wide, and covered. It had a framework on both sides and the front that would allow it to be screened, if so desired. Rick just hadn't had time for that project since they had built the place. It had a swing at the south end. It was like one from Ed's childhood. It was hung from the ceiling of the porch roof and squeaked when swung. There were several old-style rockers on the porch, one specifically for Ed. Placed tastefully along the length of the porch were pots—some large, others small—filled with various types of plants.

Rick had done really well since the downsizing of the family farm. He had bought into his uncle's hardware business. With his uncle's age, and Rick's commitment to the farm, they had sold off most of the store chain. Rick was able to use his natural business ability to make this one store the focal point for many of the farmers in the area. That single store, even with the threat of a soon-coming Wal-Mart, was doing good business. Well known and respected in the entire area, folks, especially farmers, would drive from towns as far as one hundred miles away just to trade. Ed smiled as he recalled when he was a kid and old Mr. Jones and his sons had a store on that same location. In fact, some of the buildings were the same. But they sold and traded in mules and horses. Now, Rick did sort of the same things, but with tractors.

With his dad's failing health and waning years, Rick and his wife, Liz, had insisted that Ed live out his time with them. They had bought the old home place where Ed had grown up. In fact, the place had been in the family for well over one hundred years. The old house itself was gone, with its outside toilet and well. The new one, large, modern, and designed by Rick and Liz—with some suggestions from Ed—stood proudly in its place. Ed had really hated to see the old house, as run down as it was from many years of use, torn down. It had been repaired so many times over the years until, like Ed, it finally got to the point of being beyond repair. But the huge cottonwood tree Ed and his brother had played under as children was still standing strong. Ed would often sit in his rocker and visualize he and the others—brother, friends, and cousins—playing under the old tree so many years ago. Ed was so thankful to the Lord that he had not been cursed with that terrible disease that had stricken so many of his friends: Alzheimer's. He was able to recall details of his past life, as well as what happened yesterday.

He would think about his brother, who had departed this earth several years ago, as had the love of his life, Susan. He would often remember how she had suffered for so long. How his heart hurt for her as she lay suffering, and he could do nothing but pray. There were times when he would get mad at God for allowing this. Then, he would remember it was not God who put things like this on us. It was just part of the fall and sin of man. He remembered the look of peace on Susan's beautiful face when, at last, she was released to go home. Now, he wanted to do the same. But he had been so hurt to see her go. Even though he had his son and his family close by, he sometimes felt alone. He was the last of the "clan." Oh, his descendants would go on, but he was the last of his generation.

He enjoyed life as much as was possible here with his family. They were strong Christians and spent a lot of time working in the small Baptist church where Rick was youth minister. Ed went every time he could. He felt at home with others his own age. However, as the months went by, there were fewer and fewer of them left. So far this year, four of the oldsters he had enjoyed playing checkers with had gone home. And it was only July. Would he be next?

Slowly he rose from his chair and reached for his cane. He moved toward the steps. As he approached the bottom step, he reached out with his right leg (the stronger of the two) and planted it firmly on the ground. He always had a certain dread that he would not be properly set and balanced when he stepped out with his weak leg. There had been a slight stroke involved with one of the heart attacks, and it would be rather easy for him to lose his balance and fall.

As he stepped onto the ground, he felt an all too familiar pain in the middle of his chest. Remembering the major heart attack he had suffered five years ago, and the two lighter ones since, he stopped short and sat down on the middle step of the porch. When the doctor checked out his "plumbing," he found that virtually every pathway taking blood to his heart was stopped up. This had caused the attack and should have caused a major stroke. But God had been merciful to him and spared him that horror. Since then, he had tried to watch his diet and walked down to the old pond every day. The trip was about one hundred yards, and it would usually take a full hour. But today he just didn't feel up to it. He popped one of the small tablets into his mouth, and within a few seconds, the pain was gone. He would walk around to the back of the house, toward where the old mule barn had been. Then, if he got to feeling better, maybe move down toward the pond.

Ed loved that old pond. It was old when he was a kid. He and his brother would spend long, sunny days catching small sunfish for their mom to fry. Lot of bones, but they would be cooked so as to be soft. Often his memories would turn to the many important events of life that had taken place around that pond. Especially the old stump, looking now exactly as it did when he first saw it so many years ago. It gave him comfort and assurance. It was at that stump, so many years ago, where he first invited Jesus to be his Savior.

As Ed walked slowly toward the pond, all the thoughts of long ago filling his mind, he was suddenly hit by an elephant, right in the chest. Everything went dark. And that was the last thing he remembered.

Jesse, his oldest grandson (named after Ed's dad), happened to be getting his horse out of the lot, preparing for his daily ride down toward the pond and into the meadow on the other side. He jumped on the horse's back, deciding to ride him bareback rather than go to the trouble to saddle him. He gathered the reins in his right hand, and touching him in the ribs, the big sorrel jumped into a gallop. As he looked down toward his destination, he spotted something on the ground. Suddenly, in total panic, he realized it was a person. And it could only be Grandpa. He screamed for his mother, who was standing on the front porch, watching for his dad to come home from the store. "Mom," he yelled, "I think Grandpa is hurt."

Jesse slid the horse to a stop beside the still figure, bailing off the animal's back even before he had fully stopped. Kneeling beside the still form, he spontaneously began to pray for the old man. His mother had already called 911 before she got to his side. Ed was face-down and did not seem to be breathing. Jesse gently rolled his Granddad over on his back. A quick check confirmed that he was not breathing, and had very little pulse.

They both had studied CPR: Jesse in Scouts and Liz at a meeting at the church. Jesse began CPR at once, while his mom called his dad at the store.

Ed had been a father to Liz for the twenty-five years she and Rick had been married. Her dad had died when she was only three years old, and she never had the blessing of a strong male figure in her life. Ed had provided that! She was not ready to give him up. He was unconscious and not breathing, but Jesse got him back!

Ed's Last Moments

Ed lay in the hospital bed. Tubes ran from needles in his arms to bottles filled with fluids. Other tubes ran from his nostrils to the oxygen plug, located on the wall behind the bed. He struggled to suck in enough air to fill his tired old lungs at least partially. Each breath was labored and heavy. Occasionally, his chest would lie still for what seemed like too long. Then he would jerk, gasp, and start the labored breathing again. He was dying. His family knew it. The doctor knew it. The nurses knew it. And Ed knew it. The family had agreed that he be kept comfortable, with no attempt to revive him should his heart stop again. His heart kept trying to quit, and the miracle of modern medicine would start it back. All had agreed, including Ed, that when it stopped again, he would be allowed to pass on.

In his semi-conscience state, Ed began to reflect on his life. He knew his time in this life was short, and in the quietness of his inner self, with his mind alert, he wanted just to remember.

Let's visit Ed as he waits for the final moment.

I have seen eighty-five—no, eighty-six—birthdays. I am dying. In fact, I may be only a few minutes from death. Seems my heart just keeps stopping. Then the doctor will start it back. As I understand it, my family has told them to just make me comfortable and not start my heart back the next time it quits. I guess I am in agreement with that. I am in what might be called a holding pattern, just waiting for the end.

As I lie here in this hospital bed, with just enough things hooked up to keep me comfortable, I feel totally alone. I had heard somewhere that when it comes your time to die, you will die totally alone. It matters not that your family may be gathered around. During the death of my wife, Susan, the entire family was gathered close around her bedside until the end. I hoped that all of us being close to her might make any sense of aloneness she may feel go away. But now I can see what they were talking about. Even though there is always one or more of my family members close by the bed, I still am totally alone. At least, that's the way I feel.

I'm not in pain now. That's good! I thought my mind would be sort of numbed down, but my thinking seems to be really clear. That may be good … maybe not. Am I scared? You bet! Well … maybe not terrified but

highly concerned. See, I really don't know what happens after death. Know what? Neither does anybody else—at least not for absolutely sure.

As I lie here, my thoughts drift to what I have heard about death. I suppose, like most everyone else, I really didn't put a whole lot of time into thinking about it 'til now. However, in the last few years, I have found myself thinking more about it than at any other time in my life. It always seemed to be sort of ... out there. Now I'm right at death's door, and I really don't know how I feel about that.

I reach out with my mind to those times when I did put some thought into dying, like when I first invited Jesus Christ to be my Savior. I was nine or so, I think. We lived on the same farm where my ancestors have lived for over one hundred years and where I live with my son and his family now. Out in back of the house was a large pond. I can see it now! Every so often, my dad would host a youth campout there with neighborhood kids and kids from the church. There would always be some sort of preacher there to tell us about Jesus. I remember this one campout. Brother Malcolm, our pastor, was there, and he gave us what he called the plan of salvation. I had heard it a lot of times before in church and during our family prayer times. A lot of the kids went down to pray the sinner's prayer, and I really felt it was my time. I remember that, when I prayed that prayer, there was a peace that sort of wrapped around me. My dad wanted to make sure I understood what I was doing. He certainly wanted my brother and I to accept Christ but not to just go through the motions because somebody else did. Mom was sure I was ready and thought it was great. When I think about all the things that happened during my childhood, I sure miss Mom and Dad. I wonder if I will know them when I get to heaven. I have heard it both ways from different preachers. Guess they really don't know either.

Then there was Susan. She and her family moved to our area from Birmingham when I was about sixteen years old. We met at church, thanks to Irma, her second cousin and a born matchmaker. She had long black hair and blue eyes. She lived just far enough away to go to a different school. But we were together every weekend at church. By the time we entered high school, we were madly in love. I remember that in those days, dating consisted of sitting on the front porch in the swing, and maybe, just maybe, if the old folks went inside, holding hands. Most of the time we would just sit together on the porch swing at her house or mine, talking about the future. I was one year ahead of her in school.

I turned nineteen in 1942. The war was really starting to churn, so I joined. Just over a year after my enlistment, I had been captured by the Nazis and spent the next two years in a POW camp. Life was pretty rough. Those were not nice people. Most of the guys I was locked up with were grunts, and we had nothing important to tell the enemy. So we just had to work, building roads, repairing the prison, and so on. Hard work, dirty, crappy food, but they kept us busy.

I remember one guy, Henry something, who had been youth pastor at his church before joining up. He was really concerned about the spiritual condition of us all. He would hold Bible studies. And for the most part, the Nazis just left him alone. Most of them were really not against religion, at least not at the guard level.

It was after one of the daily Bible studies Henry conducted with whoever would sit and listen. He talked about what Christianity was really all about. He had such a unique way of explaining God's plan. It sounded so practical … so un-religious. That was the first time I had ever heard it explained quite that way. I know that I had heard it from our pastor, as well as from my mom and dad. But this time, it really seemed to take root. Since joining the army, I had done some things that I would never have believed I would do. I remember feeling I needed something far beyond what I had experienced as a kid around that campfire, especially considering what I was going through now. We all knew that we could die any day. We had been told that if the allied troops broke through the German lines, located some twenty kilometers away, we would all be shot before we could be rescued or escape. Along with several other guys, I knelt and asked Christ to forgive me and totally take over my life. Oh! And please get me home safe! I don't know whether I was really getting born again then or just rededicating my life. But Jesus answered both my prayers.

A few weeks later, our guys hit that compound so fast and efficiently, until it was all over before the Nazis could lift a finger to kill us. If fact, I remember that they just high tailed it out of there as soon as they heard the Americans coming. I remember one guy named Tim, who had been one of my closest friends. He had laughed at Henry and cursed God. That scared me more than the guards. I didn't hear from Tim after we were liberated. But when we were set free, he pointed his finger at me and said, "See, Ed, you old holy-roller. We got rescued, and we didn't even need God for it. Only our troops! All you praying Joes were wasting your time." He's probably dead by now, as are most of those guys. Maybe I'll be seeing some of them soon.

When I was set free and got to a radio, I contacted my folks. I remember I had forgotten the phone number, but a chaplain at the MASH hospital where I was recovering was able to get it for me. Mom told the pastor who had visited with them to let them know I was alive that Dad had gotten killed in a tractor accident the year before. My heart broke. Because of the way I had acted before leaving for the war, the old guilt came back. I was really hurting. I even tried to blame God for it. Well, that foolishness didn't last long. The fact that I had acted like a fool wasn't His fault. It was all mine! So I accepted it, asked forgiveness, and moved on.

I remember that Mom was still teaching Sunday school at the small church. She said they had written me several letters, telling me they were praying for me. I never got any of them. The Nazis made sure we never got anything positive from home. She told me that Susan had waited for me, certain I would return. We got married about six months after I got home. I lost her a bit over ten years ago now. When that happened, my life pretty much ground to a halt. I am looking forward to seeing her shortly. I really don't know what I am saying, but it is a really comforting thought.

I refocused on my present dilemma. Was what I had done that day in the POW camp enough? Was all I had believed enough, or was it even the truth? What if those people who claim there is no God are right, and the Christians are wrong. From where I am today, that could be a very important question. Or does it really matter at this point in time? Is it normal to have these kinds of questions as you stand at the door of death? It is a little late to be asking the question, but it sure seems relevant to what seems is about to happen to me. Will it all be nothing but darkness ... forever? Will I just go to sleep for all the time between now and what I have been told about a future resurrection? Does it really matter? I remember standing at Susan's grave and asking myself, "Is she still here, in some way, with her body? Is she asleep somewhere?" All this is so hard to understand! My mind reaches for a strange thought. Every person who was alive in the entire world when I was born and who was, say, twenty-five years old, has gone through some sort of death experience. How did they feel? Were they asking the same questions I am asking? That is, if they had time.

Just to be sure, I asked Jesus to come into my heart and prepare for this soon coming event. Suddenly, I was overcome by peace. Boy, what peace! I sure never expected this. I thought there would be a lot of fear and pain. Maybe the painkiller stopped the pain. It may have sort of numbed my mind. But my thinking seems clear. In fact, I seem to be able to think clearer than I can ever remember. I can sense others in the room, close to me. Who's there? I can see you! Is that my son and his family? Please … come closer. If I am about to go, I want to see your faces one more time. Why are you all dressed in white suits? Oh! I know. This is not my family. These are some of those student nurses, all gathered around to see me die. But nurses today don't wear white. Why is everything getting so bright? Why are they turning all the room lights up so high? Turn them down! I have never seen lights so bright.

I sense an enveloping of peace and power. Never have I felt anything like this. Slowly, I become aware of a strange change taking place. I am looking down at my body. A nurse runs over to my bed. I can hear the heart monitor send out its steady alarm sound. I see my son drop down on his knees beside the bed. Rick asks Jesus to receive me into his care. He tells me good-bye! I am overcome with a peace and sense of power like nothing I can describe. Suddenly, all is like a white light explosion, and the room and all in it disappear from sight.

Meet Timothy Edwards

Tim's Life Begins

BEVERLY EDWARDS LAY ON THE hard bed in the maternity ward of the Chicago Charity Hospital. It was June 2, 1924. She would remember that date, because it was sure to be the worst day of her miserable life. The one thing she did not need was a baby. She did not want the baby. She hated it even before it was born. She had tried to give herself an abortion. She couldn't even do that right. Now, here she was. In terrible pain! Facing life with a brat she already hated. She didn't even know for sure who the father was. The worthless bum she was married to wasn't sober long enough to get her pregnant. But there had been several other men who paid her for her favors. so she could keep enough dope to stay sane.

Somebody walked into the room and up to her bedside. He wore the telltale collar of a priest. Of all the things she needed less than a baby, this freak was it. He made some sort of a sign over her. She slapped at his hand and cursed him and his God. He asked her if she was Catholic. "Hell no!" she snapped. "What's God ever done for me?" He asked if he could pray for her and her baby. Then he started to babble on, without waiting for her to answer. She stuck both her fingers in her ears and cursed as loudly as she could while he prayed. With that, the priest exited the room.

Beverly lay there, contemplating her life. She had been born in Joplin, Missouri. She very seldom saw her dad, because he worked all the time. He was determined to make a good living for his family. Result? He and her mother fought all the time. And as if that wasn't enough, her dad was convinced that she was no good and would turn out to be a whore if he didn't keep a tight rein on her. She had to sneak out of the house to be with any of her friends. Then, when he caught her, he would beat her with his belt until she was almost unconscious. She had finally had enough. One night, just after her sixteenth birthday, she tiptoed into her mom and dad's bedroom. She knew it was payday, and her dad would have most of his money in his wallet. Quietly, she slipped his wallet out of his pants, which were hanging on the bedpost, and removed the money. It was almost dawn, so by the time she had walked into town, it was about time for the only train that passed though Joplin to arrive. She bought a ticket to Chicago. Once she got there, she knew her dad could not come after her. From there, she would decide where she would go next.

Over the next five years, she worked her way from one side of town to the other, as well as to several small Illinois towns. She tried repeated to escape the horrible life she was living trapped in the big city. But each time she was forced back to the same lifestyle just to survive. During that time, she did about everything imaginable to make money to stay in some fleabag apartment and to get her next fix. Every so often, she would buy something to eat. She had lived with several men. She had been beaten, arrested, abandoned on the side of desert roads and mistreated in about every way she could imagine. It seems she had made one bad decision after another. Finally, she met Frank in a bar on the south side of Chicago. He seemed to be an answer to a prayer. That is, if she had every thought about praying about her dilemma. He had a good job, a nice little apartment, and no ties. So, when he invited her to move in with him, she jumped at the chance. That was three years ago. Things were okay for the first year. Then he started to drink every day after work. Then he started going to work drunk. Then he was fired. And then he started just staying at home, using what money he could steal from Beverly to stay drunk all day. And somehow, she turned up pregnant. She had gotten a pretty good job as a waitress at a high-class bar. She had to take the streetcar to work, because the bar was in a better part of town than where she lived. Through hard work she had been moved from waitress to barmaid. Her goal was to be trained as a bar tender. But when she started to show, she was fired. The bar owner said he didn't have any use for a pregnant barmaid. And to top it all off, Frank had suddenly decided to pack his few belongings and take off for who knows where.

And now, here she was!

The bleeding had started about two weeks ago. At first, she refused to allow herself to get upset. She had tried to abort the baby herself. All she had accomplished was pain. She had tried to find somebody who would do it for her. There were no medical facilities around that would do this. She had gotten the name of a black lady who occasionally did such things … for a rather large fee. So, she was stuck with having the baby, unless she could do something that would cause the abortion. She had hoped the bleeding was a good sign. But the pain had gotten so bad that she had been forced to check into this government-run clinic. It was dirty, and the nurses who worked there most likely were too sorry to get a good job in a reputable hospital. As far as she could tell, there was only one doctor for all these people. In the same ward with her were not only other pregnant women but some people with diseases that were obvious, mainly tuberculosis.

So, she waited, and she hurt. They gave her very little for the pain. And then it happened. The pain came in horrible waves. She felt as though she was going to split open. She screamed for someone. Finally, one of the nurses wandered in, saw that Beverly was in trouble, and called the doctor. Two orderlies came in, pushing a bed with wheels, sort of threw her onto it, and headed down the hallway. They hit two swinging doors at the end of the hall, knocking them open and scraping Beverly's arm in the process. The nurse stuck a needle in her arm, telling her that it would numb the pain, but she needed to be awake so she could help them get the baby out. All Beverly wanted to do was die.

But, like most things, good or bad, it was soon over. She was only slightly aware of the loud cry of the baby when the doctor smacked him on the behind. She was cleaned up and wheeled back to her ward bed. Exhausted, she drifted off to sleep.

She wasn't sure how long she was asleep, but she was awakened by someone shaking her shoulder. She opened her eyes, and there he was. The nurse was holding the tiny bundle. She gently laid him in her arms, and Beverly fell in love. She immediately knew she could not give him up, no matter what.

And so it was that little Timothy Edwards came into this world on the "wrong side of the tracks" in Chicago, Illinois. From the start, it seemed his life was doomed to hard times.

In a few days, he and his mother left the hospital. A friend she had worked with at the bar had heard about her desperate situation and offered to help. Not that she had much to give, but she felt sorry for Beverly. The hospital had asked her how she intended to get home. She had given them her friend's address. They had gotten in touch with her, telling her when Beverly would be discharged. Her friend's name was Alice, and she had walked the twenty blocks from her apartment to the hospital. Then, she paid for the three of them to ride the streetcar back to her tiny place. Beverly would stay there for the next six weeks, until she could hopefully get some sort of work. But after only about three weeks, she was able to get work (ten hours per day) in a clothing factory. Workers were so badly needed the owner allowed her to bring her baby to work with her, placing him in a small basket next to her workstation. It was hard, but she was surviving.

It was shortly after that her husband, Frank, returned to the area and started looking for her. He went to the bar where she used to work and where he spent a lot of time drunk. Alice happened to be working that day and brought him up to date on all that had happened. He had returned to the apartment where they used to live as soon as he had gotten to town. The place was locked up, because the landlord had no idea where Beverly had gone or what to do with their personal effects that were left there. Frank had paid the rent up to date. Somehow, he had come into some money. Beverly never did find out exactly how or how much was involved. But she was glad to be able to give Alice a break and move back into her own apartment. It seemed that Frank wanted to patch things up and try to make their marriage work. However, he didn't seem to be all that excited at having a kid. That would become evident as the days and years passed.

It wasn't long until things with Frank returned to how they were before he left and Tim was born. The difference was that he did seem to be able to turn up with a fair amount of money. Problem was that he generally blew most of the money he had gotten from wherever. He returned to his lifestyle as a drunk, and he began to abuse Tim. Also, some two years after Tim was born, along came another baby. From as far back as his memory would work, Tim could remember hearing his dad curse his mom, claiming that Jeff (his younger brother) wasn't his. He also remembered the unspeakable things suffered at the hands of his father. These things that no child should experience were generally followed by beatings that left him bruised and terrified. He remembers being relieved when his father's attentions turned from him to his younger brother. He remembers his mother running him out into the street while she "entertained" strange men in their tiny home, set just off an alley on the south side of town. These events would sometimes take place while his dad was passed out drunk in another part of the house. Tim would often be awakened from a fitful sleep by gunshots, yelling, and the sound of police sirens. This was his world at the beginning of his life on earth.

When he was just nine years old, his father was killed in a barroom fight. His mother's response: "Thank God. Now maybe we can get some help from the government." Frank had never provided anything but the most basic of the family's needs. The money he contributed usually came from sources unknown to Beverly. She pretty well knew that it was not honest money. But, she really didn't care as long as there was money for the rent and boos. Most of whatever he could make was spent on his own whisky before any food was bought for the family. But now even that was gone. Tim thought things were tough before, but that was nothing compared to conditions now. Each month was a fight just to stay in the tiny house. He was old enough now to know how his mother generally paid the rent. Food was another story. When the pantry was empty, she would drag him and his brother down to the closest soup kitchen or mission to get something to eat. Occasionally, some people would bring by some bread and canned goods, and they could eat for a few more days.

As time passed, his mother began to choose to entertain men rather than go to work in one of the many factories located within bus range of their house. She said that type work was below her status. Seems some of the men who regularly visited her were beginning to pay her more for her "favors," giving her an arrogance the boys had not seen before. Shortly, Tim was spending more time on the streets than at home. This, of course, led to his becoming involved with some "friends" who introduced him to new ways to make money. Result: he soon had pockets of money to take care of his own needs. Occasionally he would give his mother a small amount of money. All this did was cause her to demand that he bring home more money. Her need for alcohol and drugs steadily increased. For Tim….his need for alcohol, drugs, and women continued to rise.

Occasionally, as he ran the seedy streets of the ghetto, he would pass by some mission. He would hear the folks inside singing. Sometimes he would stop and listen. If he listened long enough, the singing would end, and the singers would begin to file out of the church. They didn't look to be any better off than he was: at least not with physical things. But there was a difference in how they looked in the face. They would usually be smiling, hugging each other, and generally happy. What did these people have that made them that way? War was looming on the horizon, there was no money, and crime was all around, so what was the deal? On one occasion, the guy who seemed to be in charge crossed the street to where Tim was standing. Tim was always ready for a conversation with a stranger. Can't ever tell what it may turn into. Might even be a new drug supplier or maybe a buyer. Tim was still small time, but things were picking up. "Hey, Preacher Man," the conservation started with Tim.

The man stopped and turned toward Tim. He was a bit hesitant to come too close, as such an approach often turned into a robbery … or worse. But Preacher Dan took the chance. He walked toward Tim and extended his hand. Tim refused to accept his offer. Preacher Dan spoke, "How you doin' young man?"

Tim offered no answer. Instead, he asked a question. "What goes on in the building?"

"Oh, just some singing and talking."

"What do you talk about? I can hear the singing about God and stuff."

"We talk about the stuff in the Bible." Preacher Dan began to explain to Tim about becoming a Christian and going to heaven when he died. Although Tim had no interest in dying any time soon, this sparked a chord of interest. Tim had never heard of anything like that. All he had ever heard about Jesus was how his old man used to use His name when he was mad and cussing out him and his brother. He thought it was just another cussword. What the preacher said seemed to be something really good. When he asked the preacher what he would need to do to have that kind of good feeling, he was told that, to begin with, he must give up all his sinful ways. That would be the only way he would be acceptable to God. As quick as Tim had become interested, all the interest fled. He was not interested in giving up his income from drugs, his friends, or his lifestyle just to be able to smile and sing religious songs.

One night, he and two friends decided to hold up a drugstore. They were running low on drugs and felt this would be an easy way to replenish their supply. Little thought was given to what would be the result if they got caught. Also, since none of them had a car (or in those days, a horse), they decided to hotwire one parked close to the target of choice, using it for the getaway. They would hit the store just before closing time. There were several joints in the area, so there would always be several cars to choose from—as well as horses, if worse came to worse.

Tim had watched as another friend (an adult criminal) had stolen a car. He had shown Tim how to hotwire one of the old Fords. Some of the other makes were a bit trickier to do in a hurry. Time would be important during this caper. There were times when there were more horses on the streets than cars, but stealing a horse for the getaway was nuts. The job would be at night, and there were very few horses out then. Besides, cars were getting more plentiful, and making the escape in a shiny, new, horseless carriage was more exciting than the holdup.

After a couple of days casing the drugstore, Tim and his buddies felt they were ready for the holdup. One of the guys, Stevie, had stolen his dad's old Colt revolver. That would be the only weapon. While Stevie and Pedro (the youngest of the threesome) went into the store and held up the druggist, Tim would hotwire the car that had been pre-chosen and be ready to start it as soon as they came out of the store. It would take place about 8 p.m., just after dark and a few minutes before closing time for the store.

Since this was the first such activity for any of the three, all were extremely nervous. As they arrived across the street from the store, they spied the car that would be their getaway. It was an early Ford Model B. It was a beaut. Tim could hardly wait to fire it up. At the appointed time, Stevie and Pedro entered the store. Tim slipped over to the car, opened the cloth door, and got in. He sat behind the wheel and prepared for the time of his life. He just couldn't wait. He leaned over and stuck his head under the dash. This was the perfect choice for their escape vehicle, as it was one of the few with an electric starter. That meant they didn't need to crank the motor to get it started. He quickly found the two wires that needed to be tied together. With his pocketknife, he cut the two sets of wires and skinned back the insulation to expose the wires that must be tied together. As he did so, the two wires accidentally touched. Suddenly, the engine roared to life. Tim jumped. That was too quick. His two partners had not yet finished their work in the store. He was just starting to recover from the shock of the early start when the owner came running out of a doorway that led to a small café. And ... wouldn't you just know it? He had a gun in his hand, barrel pointed right at Tim's head. At about the same time, Stevie and Pedro came running out of the drugstore. They had heard the roar of the engine and panicked. It took only a split second for them to see what was taking place with Tim. They did a quick spin and fled down the alley, back toward their own part of town, leaving Tim to deal with the irate owner.

The car owner held Tim at gunpoint until the police arrived. Tim was placed under arrest and would spend the next two years in jail. While there, he would get an advanced education in how to be a really successful criminal.

After serving only eighteen months, Tim was called before the judge. It was early 1942, Japan had bombed Peril Harbor, and the war in Europe was just heating up. American troops had landed in Britain in January, and the army was scrambling to build up the troop numbers. Judges were offering to let troublemakers out of jail early on the condition they enlist in the army. That sounded like a good deal to Tim. So, off he went to boot camp.

Tim finished basic and was assigned to the 151st Field Artillery Battalion. On January 15, 1942, Tim and hundreds of other soldiers boarded the troop ship *Strathaird*, bound for Belfast, North Ireland. They arrived on January 26. In those twelve days, Tim experienced more misery than he had in all his short life. The only boat he had ever been on was a canoe at North Pond in Chicago. He and his buddies used to go there just to cause trouble. That involved getting into a canoe so they could sneak up on couples and cause them to capsize. But this ship! It seemed longer than a city block. When the seasickness finally became more than he could control, Tim would stand on what was called the fantail, head hanging over the edge, giving up all that was inside him. Then, when there was nothing left, he would turn and face forward, attempting to still the rocking mentally. From this view, the ship seemed longer than from W. 135th street on the south side of Chicago all the way to Calvary Cemetery on the north side. And it seemed the entire ocean was moving up and down. This, or course, made the ship seem to stand first on its tail and then, just as suddenly, drop on its nose. And every time this happened, Tim's stomach would swap ends from his feet to the top of his head. And once again, he would be forced to face aft, hang over the fantail, and go through the entire agonizing action again. He did a lot of praying during those times: praying he would die!

During one of the few times when the sea was somewhat calm and the ship would sort of settle down, allowing his stomach to do the same, he began to talk to some of the other guys on board. One of them was sort of a hick. His name was Ed something or other. He was from Tennessee. He also did some real praying during the rough times, but he prayed for the guys who had it so bad. The tossing and turning didn't seem to bother him as much as many of the others. Tim had never met anyone like Ed. On several occasions, they would climb up on some tanks or other heavy equipment lashed on the deck and talk. After a while, they began to share some things about their lives back in the States. Of course, Tim would rant and rave about his plight in life and brag about the mean things he had done. But it was different with Ed. He would talk about his family and life on the farm. The life he talked about was totally foreign to Tim. It sounded so tame ... so boring ... yet strangely pleasant. Then one day, Tim decided to try and find out why Ed seemed so cool with all this. They were both sitting on top of one of the tanks lashed to the deck. "Hey bub [everyone was bub to Tim at first], what is it with you? All these guys, including me, are scared, mostly sick, and cussing the whole deal. But you ... well, you seem different. Why?" For a long time, Ed gazed out at the gently rolling sea. He formed his answer carefully. That was because all the guys, include Tim, had seen his bad side. How could he answer him when he felt that his "good side" had faded away back in basic? Tim interrupted his thoughts. "What ... got no answer?"

"Tim, there was a time not so long ago when I could have given you a good answer. But now ... To begin with, I am no better than any of you guys. What I do have that gives me the edge when things get rough I have sort of backed away from. That doesn't mean that it is gone … just sort of covered up. But it all has to do with my Christian faith."

"You mean all that Jesus stuff?" Tim asked.

"Well yes!" Ed began to tell Tim how he had given his life to Christ years ago. But he was quick to explain how, under certain conditions, a person can act so differently, sort of like folks who don't believe. It's called backsliding.

Tim told Ed about his one encounter with a preacher and the gospel message. "There was this guy back home: Preacher Dan they called him. He had a small church not far from where I used to live. The people who went there would always be singing and yelling. But they were different … sort of like you are different when you're not—what did you say—backslid. So, one day I decided to ask the guy in charge what that was all about. He told me that before God would accept me, I would have to clean up my act and stop all the sinning. Well, that ended it for me. First place, I knew that was impossible. Second, why would I want to? I had all the money, drugs, liquor, and women I needed. But tell me, if I must clean up my act before God will have anything to do with me, how are you still on speaking terms with the guy upstairs?"

That really hit Ed where it hurt. "All I can say is that Preacher Dan was wrong. At least as far as I can understand it. If I could clean myself up, and further, stay that way, why do we need God? The reason He has provided salvation for us it that we can't clean ourselves up."

"Guess I'll wait and watch," Tim answered. And with that, he hopped down off the tank and trotted off toward a crap game that was going on down the deck a ways.

Finally, the troop ship with its cargo arrived at the Belfast port. It took several days to offload all the equipment. Once that was done, the troops were given several days of free time before shipping out for who knows where. Tim and many of the others were drunk within the first two hours after being turned loose. Tim looked for Ed, to ask him to join him, but he was nowhere to be found.

As a grunt, Tim and others like him weren't told much about what was happening. They were just expected to jump when shouted at. But finally, and all too soon, their ship-out day arrived. They first boarded a C-47

Skytrain. This flying troop hauler had been activated earlier that year. The thing even smelled brand new. This was the first flying experience for most of the foot soldiers. Tim found he really took to this aviation stuff. His "sort of" buddy, Ed, ended up on the same plane as Tim. They sat across from each other on the canvas seats that ran the entire length of the sides of the fuselage. Dressed in full battle gear, there was little moving around the airplane.

All too soon, the plane started its descent into some place in France. If anyone on board had any idea where they were, they didn't let on. With a bump and a couple of squeals from the tires, they were on the ground.

The next several weeks were a swirl of noise, smoke, instinctive shooting at targets you could not see, and long hours of marching, followed by short nights in the mud and cold. Just as constant were the blown-apart bodies of guys you may have just been talking to a short time before combat. Gradually, you would harden to all the pain and death, wondering if the next round would have your name on it.

Wherever they were, it was in the middle of winter, and the snow seemed to fall constantly. Slowly, their numbers dwindled, as more and more of them became the recipients of the enemy's bullets.

Tim must have been in this fight for some six weeks, when he and several other men were selected for a special recon mission. They were to scout for some heavy enemy activity. Shortly after they left on the mission, they got cut off from the main force. In other words, the enemy was between them and their home base. It happened so suddenly, they were caught totally by surprise. At one point, there were other soldiers all around them. And then, they were alone. It turned out that the "others" they had been seeing were actually enemy soldiers, and they were surrounded. They were shouted at in what had come to be recognized as German. With no choice but to drop their rifles and surrender, the Americans were quickly bound and marched off through the trees.

The trip to what was to be their home for the next two years seemed to take forever. It involved a forced march to a small train siding, then what seemed to be several days crammed into a stinking cattle car. To Tim and the others, there would be days when they would not be sure whether they were alive or dead. Their minds became numb to all around them. Most days, they didn't care. Each day was filled with its own horrors. They would dig ditches to bury their buddies who had not made it through the night. They would often hope the next hole to be dug would be theirs. Each day would be taken up with hard labor. Most of what they did made no sense. They would dig a trench in one direction, only to fill it in the next day and re-dig it in another direction.

One of those who had been here since the first was Ed, the guy Tim had first gotten acquainted with on the trip over. Occasionally, when things got to the point they seemed unbearable, Tim would consider asking Ed more about his faith. He and the few others who claimed to be Christians seemed to be able to bear up under the stress better than those who spent their time cussing God for causing all this. But it always seemed that the time was just not quite right. Days melted into weeks, which melted into months and finally into two years.

Then, suddenly, they were released. It was early one morning when American troops burst into the camp. They had heard shots from quite a distance away. As the shooting came closer, their captors began to load equipment into trucks. Then, with a few roars of the big truck engines, they were gone. When the American soldiers burst into the compound, not a shot was fired. Within a short time, trucks with the familiar star on the side started to arrive. They had all sorts of supplies on them. They first took care of the most critical medical needs and then passed out clean clothes and food—plenty of edible food. It had been nearly two years since Tim had seen an American soldier with a gun. It was a welcome sight.

Once home, Tim would continue his dysfunctional lifestyle. It seems he had learned very little from his time in the army. There were opportunities available, such as education and such, but Tim chose to go back to the streets of Chicago, with the idea of living out his life there. He did get a job at one of the factories that had started up during the war. But he could never seem to settle into a normal lifestyle. He even tried marriage. After two children (that he knew of), he deserted his family and ended up in San Francisco. He got caught stealing a car and running from the police. Result: he spent seven years in prison.

Now let us fast-forward in time to continue our story!

The years passed quickly. Suddenly, Tim is in his sixties, seventies, and now eighties. At seventy-six, he had a major heart attack and almost didn't make it. Now, at eighty-six, his failing heart, along with other physical problems, are a constant source of anger and frustration. He is just as ornery as ever. He seems determined to make himself miserable, along with everyone who has anything to do with him.

Some years ago, he located his oldest son, who he doubts is really his son. He and his wife have a small house in the gang-infested south side of town. They have three kids—two girls and a boy—all with questionable social skills. Tim's son and daughter-in-law spend most of their off time in the bars, leaving the kids in Tim's care. But as soon as they would leave, Tim would leave, too. He figured these brats could fend for themselves. After all, what was he going to do with them except pass on the same lifestyle he had growing up?

Based solely on the suspicion that Tim had a small amount of either cash or insurance and is sure to die shortly, they invited him to stay in a small bedroom, just a little larger than a walk-in closet. This gives them someone to leave the kids with while they party. This has gone on for years. And this is where we pick up the final phase of Tim's earthly story.

Tim's Last Days

Tim sat on the edge of the old cane-bottomed chair, staring at the timeworn checkerboard. It was his move, but he was taking far too long, much to the irritation of the three other old men seated around the table. The rancid smoke, exhausted from his last exhale on the cheap cigar, floated slowly toward the ceiling. Being the hateful, irritating old reprobate that he was, he enjoyed doing anything that would irritate his "buddies," as they waited for him to make his move. He had always been that way. "If you're not careful, you'll die in that position," snapped Rod. He was an old ironworker, long retired and long devoid of any social graces. "I don't give a tinkers damn if you die. It's just that you'll probably fall over and knock over the checkerboard table." It sounded like a bit of levity, but the truth of the matter was, he meant it.

Tim shot him a look, a "signal," and a response. "Go to hell, you old bum" he replied. There were no smiles associated with either man's remarks. They could be finalists in the "cantankerous old goat of the year" competition, if there were such an event.

Tim got up slowly, still without making any move of the round disks, reached for his cane, and stumbled toward the small store counter. Between being crippled up with stiff joints and about two-thirds drunk (his usual condition by this time of day), he was never sure whether he would reach his destination upright. James, the store owner, was younger than the four old coots who sat around the checker table many hours of each day. Result: he was generally short on patience with them. Sometimes, he really grew tired of them just hanging around in the way. They spent very little money, griped about everything, stunk like stale tobacco (and other things), and occasionally drove off customers. James had bought the small country store from his uncle, when he had gotten too sick to operate it. There was only one other store in this small, poor community in south Chicago. Up to this time, the nearest Wal-Mart was several miles away. But now, there was news of a Wal-Mart coming to this part of town. *Bet they wouldn't put up with these four,* he thought.

"Gimme a fresh pack of smokes," Tim crocked. "Tired of these cheap cigars. They make me stink"

James responded as he threw down a pack of the cheapest he had, "I been thinkin' about putting up no smoking signs. You guys make it tough on the few paying customers I have."

Tim shot him a disgusted look. "Do that, and we will take our business elsewhere."

"That alone is enough reason for me to put up the sign," James snapped. "Besides, I thought your heart doctor told you that if you kept smoking, you would be dead in six months."

"That would be a relief. As least I wouldn't have to put up with you jerks or with my idiot family," Tim retorted.

"Be a relief to us all, too," James whispered under his breath.

As he tried to find the chair with his rear end, he missed, falling on the table and scattering old men and checkers all over the floor. That started a ten-minute cuss match between the four, as they slowly worked their way back to their feet, joints creaking. Tim was no longer welcome, at least not for today.

Slowly, he made his way back to his house. Or rather, his eldest son's house. When he allowed himself to reflect on his miserable life, he would often ponder the bad choices that had placed him here at this time in his life. There had been so many! But as his mind played back the years, there were so many times when he wished he had done things differently. He wasn't even sure the family he was living with was kin to him. That bugged him. He had never cared about family … whether he even had one or not. But as he aged, that, along with other things, seemed to take on new importance. As far as he could figure, he had been in the army when this guy calling himself his son was conceived. Besides, they pretty well hated each other. That doesn't seem right: that is, if they were really father and son. But then he would remember the hatred that existed between him and his old man. He and the boy's mother had met just before he shipped out and had hooked up as soon as he got back to the States. She had this kid, who was about three years old. He had been a POW for two years, plus the time in Europe before being captured. Oh well! That was what life had handed him, so he might as well make the best of it for the time he had left. Besides, this guy was the only one of his two so-called offspring who would even entertain the idea of him living with them. All Tim could do as he reflected on these things was curse the day he was born.

Tim had not felt well for several weeks. All this did was cause him to be more disagreeable. He did not like his life. In fact, he had never liked his life. His father was a drunk, and his mother was a whore. At least, that was his opinion of her. As he slowly walked toward where he was lived, his mind continued to pull up memories. He didn't know why. The thoughts just seemed to come in a flood.

After his old man died when he was about nine, he recalled how he was forced to spend time on the streets while his mother had an almost constant parade of men through the small shack they lived in. At sixteen, he and two buddies tried to rob a drug store. He was supposed to drive the get- away car. He screwed that up and got caught. Both his so-called partners left him holding the bag. Oh well! That was his life! After eighteen months, he was released to join the army. He remembered that World War II was just kicking off. He figured that would be as good a place as any to spend some time. He had no interest in any sort of patriotism. The booze he could drink and the women he could meet were his only reasons for joining. It didn't work out exactly like that. Right after basic training, he was sent to the front, was captured, and spent the entire war in a POW camp. Boy, was that some bad memories. After he was liberated and returned to the States, he was back on his wild trail. He stole a car, picked up two of his buddies, and headed across country to California. To keep money in their pockets, they committed small-time robberies. And not being too high on the smart list, they got caught, and back to jail he went. Jail in the United States sure was better than the POW camp.

Out of jail after seven years, Tim had gone through one wife and three live-ins. Out of those relationships he managed to produce at least four kids (but only two he really knew about). He had serious questions as to who the father of each one really was. All three of the women had been somewhat like his mother.

His mind, sort of running on autopilot, went back to his return to Chicago. After prison in California and his return home, he had gotten a job in one of the factories. That hadn't lasted long, and he had gotten a job at the local hardware store that was owned by a friend. He had stayed there throughout the years of his life when he wasn't in jail for something stupid or in the hospital for the same reason. After one long stretch of staying sober, and generally doing what was right, he was promoted to assistant manager over one of the departments. It wasn't a very high position, but Tim let it go to his head. He was soon demoted, because he couldn't get along with any of the employees under him. On one occasion, he popped off to one of the temps in the stockroom. This guy was an old biker type, a rather new breed since the end of the war. He put a few well-placed knots on Tim's head. The owner kept him on, letting him work as a stocker, simply because they figured he couldn't get a job anywhere else. Besides, the owner had known him all his life.

Tim had retired on Social Security when he got too sick to continue with his job. That gave him a small monthly check that only served to keep him is basic food, cigars, and a few bottles of beer. He went most of his life without knowing much about this Social Security thing. It had been enacted back in 1935. Fortunately, the guy who owned the hardware store where he had worked for several years had taken out for it. Tim remembered calling both him and the government crooks for taking money out of his check each payday. Now he was glad he had. It wasn't much, but it was better than it could have been.

During the past few years, he had hitchhiked across the country, traveling like a bum just to prove he could still do it. He had lived that way for several years after he got out of prison. He had actually enjoyed the freedom and total lack of responsibility. After all the years at a job he really did not like, why not see if he could regain the freedom of that time in his life. Because of his age and failing health, it wasn't near the fun he had remembered. In all, his life had been an adventure but a waste in nearly every way. That made him mad at the world. He had always felt he had been, "dealt a bad hand," as he called it.

Then, a little over ten years ago, he had suffered a major heart attack and almost didn't make it. He has had two other less severe attacks since then. To try and keep him alive, four bypasses were performed, and a pacemaker was installed. Now, just to survive, he is restricted from all but the lightest physical activity. When he reflected on all the events of his life (which he did more and more lately), he could sense the old resentments at his plight swell up again. But lately, there seemed to be a new, unfamiliar feeling. He had never been afraid of anything. But here he was, eighty-six, almost eighty-seven years old, full of hate, and nearly always drunk and sick. His son's family had taken him in but made it known (by their silent actions) they did not like him being there. He knew they only put up with him because they would occasionally ask him if he had a will. In order to stay there, he played along with the idea, letting them think so. He even baited them a bit. His daughter-in-law, who made no bones about how she felt about him being there, had even asked him where he had hidden his money. There was also an old insurance policy he had gotten while in the army. He had totally forgotten about it until some guy from the Veteran's Administration found a statement about it in his records. It was paid up, but he had no idea where any policy was. But the policy number and name of the company were both recorded in his records. His contact at the VA had located the company and gotten a phone number for Tim. The policy had grown over the years, so he cashed it in. He had to do all this on the sly. He figured if he got his hands on any money and his son found about it, he would probably kill him in his sleep to get it. What a deal!

On and on his mind played the recordings of the mess he had made of his life. Occasionally, he would wonder what death might be like. Would he just go to sleep, with nothing but darkness forever? Or, like some things he had heard, would he come back as someone, or something, else? Boy, if that was the case, he hoped the next one would be smarter than he had been. Then, he would just push the thoughts and questions aside, because, as far as he knew, nobody had any idea what the answer really was.

Today, as usual, he had to pass by a small church that seemed to be always open. They would feed hungry people and let them sleep in a room in the basement of the building. He had wandered in one day when he was so drunk he couldn't remember where his son's house was. That was just after he had moved in with them. They wanted to get him "saved," before they would do anything else for him … feed him or take him home. He had fixed them. He had told them all to go to hell, and he ended up sleeping on the sidewalk in front of the place. The next morning, after he had sobered up, he remembered where the house was and made his way home. He decided that was a really stupid stunt to pull, considering the neighborhood. He was surprised to be still alive in the morning. None of that bunch at home seemed to notice he had not been home all night and wouldn't have cared if they had noticed. He remember how, so many years ago, the preacher (now dead) of this same church had told him he must clean up his life before God would do anything for him. Guess the message remains the same: solve your own problems, and I might accept you. He wondered what kind of God this God was!

As he made his way home today, he detected an increasing pressure in the middle of his chest. It had started while he was playing checkers at the store. He had felt it several times before, but not this bad … not since his original heart attack. Now, it seemed to be getting worse. And he was suddenly scared. Was this the last time? Was the big day about to dawn? He saw the ground coming toward his face. Everything went black just as his head bounced off the dirt in the front yard of his son's house.

Tim's Time Has Come

Tim lay in the hospital bed. It had been three days since he had collapsed in the front yard. Now, tubes ran from needles in his arms to bottles filled with fluids. Tubes ran from his nostrils to the oxygen plug in the wall behind the bed. His breathing was labored and heavy. Occasionally, the breathing would stop for what seemed like too long. Then he would jerk, gasp, and start the labored breathing again. He was dying. His family knew it. The doctor knew it. The nurses knew it. And Tim knew it. The family had agreed that he be kept comfortable, with no attempt to revive him should his heart stop again. Tim refused to take care of himself after his massive heart attack eight years ago. Even with the additional attacks, he just would not take his mortality seriously. Now, his heart was trying to just quit, but the miracle of modern medicine would start it back. All had agreed, including Tim, that when it stopped again, he would be allowed to pass on. Why not? He had nothing for which to live.

Let's listen in on Tim's thoughts as he waits for the final moment.

Well, this may really be it. Something tells me I won't leave this place under my own power. I've seen eighty-five ... no ... eighty-six birthdays. The doctor told me point blank that I'm dying. Sort of a cold, old buzzard. Guess he's not getting enough dough out of me. If fact, he may go in the hole on me. I don't know how all this Medicare stuff works at this point. I wouldn't think they would spend all that much money on an old coot who is about to cash in. Who cares? What a joke life has been! I may be only a few minutes from death. My heart keeps stopping. Then the doctor will start it back. As I understand it, my so-called family has told them just to make me comfortable and not start my heart back the next time it quits. Wanting to make me comfortable is crap. All that bunch of losers wants is what few dollars they think I might have. Will they be ticked off when they find out that what little bit I had left in my tiny insurance policy has already been given away! I figured my time was short, and I had no intention of letting my looser "family" get their hands on it. So, I cashed the policy in almost six weeks ago and gave it all to that little mission church down the street from their house. All they will get is enough to put me in the ground. Most likely, they will bury me as a pauper so they can get drunk on the $2,000 I left for my funeral. They may even have me cremated and then flush my ashes down the toilet. Oh well! Who cares! I've lived most of my life in the sewer. I'll feel right at home. Might as well go out in the same direction.

As I lie here in this hospital bed, with most all of the stuff now unhooked, I feel like I have been totally screwed all my life. But if I'm really honest, the only person I have to blame is myself. Seems like all I've ever done is make bad decisions. Now, here I am, dying, and totally alone. I had heard somewhere that when you die, you do so totally alone, no matter how many people may be standing around, gawking at you. Now I can see what they were talking about. As far as I know, none of my family members have even been around since they decided that I was too far gone to know if they were here of not. Truth is, I didn't even care if they were here. All they do is stand around the bed and tell dirty jokes, or make fun of me for some of the things I have done. On one occasion, I even heard the pig my so-called son married ask if I had any money and did he have any idea it might be stashed. She did that right in front of me! How sorry can that be? They don't think I can hear them. But I can hear every word. They can all go to the devil, as far as I am concerned. I guess I will be waiting on them, pitchfork in hand. Seems sort of stupid to be thinking thoughts like that in my condition and all. But I have never believed in hell, heaven, Jesus, the devil, or any of those fairy tales. So why change my mind now? It's all a bunch of hype. When I go, that will be it. Nothing but darkness. With my life, that will be a relief.

At least I'm not in pain now. That's good! I thought my mind would be sort of numbed down, but my thinking seems to be really clear. That may be good … maybe not. Am I scared? You bet! Actually, terrified. Even though I have laughed at this Jesus and heaven stuff all my life, I guess deep down I still have my doubts. See, I really don't know what happens after death. Know what? Neither does anybody else, at least as far as I can tell.

I remember the first time I heard about this Jesus stuff. My folks had shipped me and my brother off to a church youth camp when I was about eight years old. That was so they could get rid of us for a weekend. I remember that there was some guy, an evangelist I think they called him, who kept harping at us about being saved. He told us about something called a plan of salvation. A lot of the kids went down to pray with this guy. In fact, my brother went down and prayed. This preacher had told them that if they did that, when they die, they would go to heaven. I wonder about my brother sometimes. I haven't seen him since before I went in the Army. When I got back he had left Chicago. I hope his life has been better than mine. What was I thinking before I started thinking about my brother? Oh yes! Well, dying was just not in my plans. I had a lot of living to do yet, and this sissy religion stuff wasn't going to mess that up.

Besides, I figured that if I came home with some cock-and-bull story about accepting Jesus as my Savior, my old man would beat the stuffing out of me. That is, after he laughed me out of the house. Know what? That is exactly what happened to my brother when he ran in and told him what had happened. The old man made him deny the entire thing before he would stop whaling on him with his belt. Mom really didn't know quite what to think about it all. She had gone to church some when she was a kid. Nope, that was not for me. But what about now? What if all that stuff is real? Boy would that make me the fool. Oh well! Too late for all that.

I do remember another time when I was almost conned into trying this "being saved" stuff again. I turned eighteen in 1942. I had been in juvenile lockup for about eighteen months for robbing a store. The war was really starting to churn, and I could get out if I joined the army. So ... I joined. Just over a year following my enlistment, I was captured by the Nazis and spent the next two years living in a POW camp. Life was pretty rough. Those were not nice people. Most of the guys I was locked up with were grunts, and we had no information of value to give to the Nazis. So, we just had to work, building roads, repairing the prison, and so on. Hard work and dirty, crappy food, but they kept us busy.

I remember one guy, Henry something, who had been some kind of minister at his church before joining up. He had been some sort of preacher before the war. Guess he still considered himself one. For the most part, the Nazis just left him alone. Most of them were really not against religion, at least not at the guard level. In fact, I suppose I was more against all the God stuff than they were.

This guy would hold these Bible meetings. Most of the time, no one was interested. It was after one of the daily Bible studies Henry conducted with whoever would sit and listen. He talked about what Christianity was really all about. That was the first time I had ever heard it explained that way: how Jesus had taken all our sins on Himself. But I still wasn't interested, even though it sounded like a good deal. I remember that several of the guys actually prayed with him. This one guy, Ed, that I had gotten to be pretty good friend with, even helped this Henry guy with the meeting. He had been one of those Bible thumpers when we first got here. But he had sort of changed during basic training. But since being here, he had "rededicated" his life, I believe he called it. That stuff was way over my head. At first, I wanted nothing to do with him because of all the religion stuff. But even with that, he was a good soldier. Sort of a plain guy. At the end of the meeting, he sort of fell down on his knees and started crying like a baby, praying for the all of us other guys and asking God to get us out of this POW camp. He even embarrassed me. We had made some real neat plans for what we were going to do after we got out—if we did. Now, I guessed that these plans were all up in smoke, with him returning so strong to his religion and all. He was from some hick town in Tennessee. His family owned a big farm or something. He had even invited me to come there and stay for a while. He had gotten on the outs with his family but said that everything would be okay once he got home (or rather, *if* he got home). But he had really flip-flopped since I first met him. First, a dyed in the wool Bible thumper, then changing to sort of become like the rest of us, and then changing back. I figured it was out of fear of dying. Me? If the Nazi pigs decided to take me out, I planned on taking as many with me as possible. After we were liberated, I never heard from Ed again. Probably dead by now. Most of the guys are. And I will be soon, I guess.

Wish someone would bring something for the pain. It comes and goes. One minute it feels like an elephant is sitting on my chest. Then it goes away, and I can breathe pretty well. Then it starts over again. I wish I had something that would just take me out. I am tired of the pain, as well as the fear. Boy, what fear! I sure never expected this. I thought there would suddenly be a lot of nothing but not all the fear and pain. Come on, death, whatever you are. Maybe the painkiller had helped for a while, but it did nothing about the fear of dying. What really will happen? What if there is a hell? Maybe if this God is as good as all the Bible thumpers claim, He will just feel sorry for me and let me into heaven, if it even exists.

I thought the painkiller would numb my mind. But my thinking seems clear. In fact, I seem to be able to think clearer than I can ever remember. I can sense somebody in the room, close to me. Who's there? I can see you! Is that my so-called family? What are they doing here? Come to put the pillow over my face? Don't you dare come any closer! If I am about to go, I don't want the last thing I see to be your ugly faces. Boy! If there is a God, I sure hate Him, making me go through all this. Where's all this love He is supposed to have? Hey! You at the foot of my bed. I can see you! Why are you all dressed in black, with your faces covered? Why are all of you surrounding my bed, trying to grab me? Get your hands off me! Turn the lights back on! Leave me alone, damn you! Everything is so black! I have never seen such blackness! I want to scream, but I can't. My voice won't work. Somebody help me! Please, God, help me! Jesus, are you there? Can't you do something? Oh God! Oh God!

The blackness swallowed him whole.

The Entrance

Ed Finds Himself in a Beautiful Place

As THE HOSPITAL ROOM EXPLODES in whiteness, the bright light slowly fades. At first, things around Ed seem ... well ... sort of normal. That is, except for the fact that Ed has never had clearness of vision like he suddenly has. As he sort of gathers his senses, he looks around. He finds himself standing on a pathway. But it is unlike anything he has ever seen or felt. He feels all over like nothing he could ever imagine, or could explain. The first thing he notices is the deep, deep sense of peace and assurance. He senses it is not a peace that is resident within him, but rather, the peace and other emotions he has never felt seem to be surrounding him, pressing in on him, permeating his very being. In return, his mind seems to reach out and embrace all that is around him. The light that seems to emanate from everything is a soft blue, but not like any blue he has ever seen. And with each passing moment, it changes. The very environment seems to throb with life and energy. The glow seems to light up everything. It's not a bright light, and it's not a low light. He can see all the details of everything around him ... even minute features.

Overlaying the pathway he is standing on are small, smooth stones that seem transparent, like crystal. They feel so good to his feet. He looks down. He is amazed and shocked to see that he has no feet. At least, none that he can see. Yet he can feel the stones. It's like they are massaging his feet. Along both sides of the path are the most beautiful flowers he has ever seen. Before, he and Susan had liked to raise roses. She had even won

61

some prizes at the county fair. But these … wow! They look to be about three feet across and were of more colors than he could ever name. He reached out to touch one of them. He could feel the texture between his fingers, but he could not see his fingers. Where was his body? He had no body! How could he? His body was lying on the hospital bed … back … wherever … dead.

As he gently stroked the surface of the flower, there was an unnamable sense of energy that seemed to enter into every part of his being. It was as if the flower was feeding him with pure strength. All he could think of to say was, "Wow!"

As he pondered these things, so new to him, he heard a noise behind him. The sound was like a … what? A whisper? No, more like a sound made up energy and praise; there was no way to express what it sounded like. The resonance coming from the sound seemed to hit him in the back and then permeate his entire being with peace and other emotions he had no name for. He turned quickly to see what—or who—had made such a sound. Nothing! As he turned back to the front, there stood a creature like nothing he had ever seen. Standing a good ten feet tall, the "whatever" was the most perfect specimen of what seemed to be a human form that he could imagine. This being (he suddenly knew that it was an angel) wore a white and gold tunic with a wide, golden belt. His shoes looked like pictures of the sandals Roman soldiers wore. His skin seemed to radiate a soft, golden glow. Ed cautiously raised his eyes in an attempt to see the being's eyes. Suddenly, he found himself looking directly into the being's eyes … level! He and the being were eye level to each other. Ed wasn't sure if he had grown taller or if the angel had grown shorter. The eyes of the celestial being seemed to have no bottom. There was wisdom, love, power, and all other sorts of emotions, most of which Ed had never experienced, emanating from those eyes. All the energy and other emotions un-nameable that Ed could see behind those eyes seemed to discharge into what was Ed's most basic being. As he gazed into the angel's eyes, he was filled, and filled, and filled still more with emotions beyond description. A smile broke across the angel's face. As if reading Ed's thoughts, he said simply that he would get accustomed to that form of spirit-to-spirit communication. It was the norm here. In answer to Ed's other silent question, the angel explained to Ed did not have a body in the sense that he had understood before. It was not, of course, the body he would have after the resurrection, but rather, a body made up of pure energy. However, it was a form of spirit body and not yet fully visible to Ed. If Ed were patient, it would progressively become visible. Suddenly he understood. As Ed grew more accustomed to his new environment, the body would slowly come into view. Since it was pure energy, however, he could use it even now, just like he used his physical body.

The angel continued to speak. "My name is Asher. I have been assigned to introduce you to your new surroundings. But first of all, may I deliver a message from the Master. 'Welcome home, and into the joy of your Lord, you good and faithful servant.'" That totally unnerved Ed. How could that be a true welcome? He had been, at best, a nominal Christian. He had believed the gospel message the best he knew how. He felt he had been really born again. But he had done nothing of any real value that he knew of. Suddenly, with his new and expanded understanding, he knew such a welcome was based not on anything he had done but on his acceptance of what the Master had done for him. His heart (wherever it was located now) seemed to melt with love and adoration for the Master, whom he was yet to see in person.

With that, Asher turned and started walking toward a huge wall. Ed had not noticed it before. In fact, as far as he could tell, it had not been there. Yet, how could he have missed it? It seemed to be at least one hundred feet tall and glowed like bronze (or maybe gold). He proceeded along behind the giant figure. He could not remember ever walking so effortlessly and with such a feeling of power and other sensations he could not name, because he had never experienced them. It may be that to describe his movement forward as walking would be inaccurate. It was more like gliding along the pathway. One thing that was so noticeable was that, of all the emotions that surged through his entire being, there was not one hint of anything negative. He had no idea that everything could be so positive.

As they continued toward the massive wall, Ed could not help but take in all that was around him. It seemed that the forest and meadows, or whatever they were, continued forever and in all directions except directly ahead. There towered the massive wall. And it stretched in both directions for as far as Ed could see. And the sky! He had never seen such crystal blue. Yet, it was not really blue as he had come to describe blue. And it was not really sky. At least, not like he was accustomed to. It was like the purest of daytime, yet he could see planets that were spread throughout the universe. He had no idea how that could be. Before, when it was daytime, even the moon wasn't visible, except under certain conditions. But here, in full daylight, it seemed the entire galaxy was clearly visible. He remembered seeing pictures that were taken by a giant space telescope. It showed massive clouds of planets. The scientists called them "developing galaxies." But never were any of the pictures like what he could now see. And he could see, it seemed, forever. There would be no way that he could describe what he saw. Yet, in some strange way, he understood what he was looking at.

Asher turned, temporarily halting his trek toward the wall. He smiled, looking up into the vastness. "That's your territory," he remarked.

That caught Ed off guard. "What do you mean?" he asked.

"Oh, you'll see!" replied the giant, looking down at Ed like a wise teacher might look at a hungry student about to receive a morsel of knowledge. With that, he turned and continued toward the wall.

Tim's Arrivals at His Destination

Timothy Is Horrified at Where
He Is and What He Sees

As THE UGLY DARKNESS THAT gathered around his deathbed fades into blotchy blackness tinted with red flashes, Timothy is surprised to find himself standing in the middle of what looks like a pathway. It is unlike anything he has ever encountered in life. It personally feels like nothing he has ever even imagined: nothing he has language to explain. The first thing he notices is that the pathway is covered with what looks like red-hot coals. The next thing he notices is the excruciating pain he feels in his feet. The horrid pain slowly radiates all the way to the top of his head, or what he thinks is his head. It suddenly dawns on him that he is barefoot and standing in hot coals. The next thing is that the air is like molten metal. He seems to be wrapped in the burning heat. The pain is unbearable. He tries to lift one foot at a time out of the burning coals, but this does not lessen the pain. He senses a deep, deep awareness of horror and aloneness. He realizes, somehow, that he is not really alone but is in a place that is totally hostel to everything he is as a being. All the horror that envelops him seems to reach out and wrap itself around him with fiery tentacles. He is conscious of other creatures around him. He cannot actually see them, but he can sense them. They seem to squeeze in on him, scattering some nameless horror into his consciousness. In addition, his actual core seems to be reaching out to accept the horror. He tries to resist this but cannot.

The radiance, if you can call it that, is a sickening crimson blaze, saturated with traces of green and other colors he cannot recognize. The sight seems to produce a deep nausea that pervades his entire person.

The agony he feels in his feet and legs only grows worse. He has experienced the pain of having his skin scorched: he remembers being burned in an accident at work. That seems so far away, yet vivid in his memory. What he is suffering here in this damnable place, whatever it is, seems to be millions of times crueler, with a malevolent presence. Before, he remembers that when the pain of the burn was the most terrible, his mind would deaden the sensation of agony slightly, making it endurable. Not so here. It seems that his mind is struggling to help make the pain grow worse. He wants to scream, but he seems to have no mouth through which to deliver the sound. Yet, he can feel what seems to be a body much like what he had on earth. He looks down, realizing again that he has no feet. At least none he can see! What he observes are red, smoldering stubs where his legs and feet used to be. No! Burning stumps are not the way to describe them. He remembers seeing electrical wires shorted out and how they would began to glow red. That's more like what his legs look like. Even in his tormented state, he knows that the body he has known so long is still lying on the hospital bed. So what is this?

All along the borders of the flaming pathway stands what look like burning trees. He can barely make out the silhouettes in the enraged darkness. But they look like trees that are on fire, yet not being consumed. His mind suddenly screams at him that he is the same way. He is some sort of intelligent substance, on fire yet not being consumed. An unnamable panic rises up and envelops his entire mind. It seems that each of the fiery stones under where his feet should be can be felt and emits its own brand of burning hell.

He has an overpowering passion to reach out and touch one of the flaming trees. As he does, he jerks back in pain. They are like molten steel. He felt the burn, even though he could see no arm or hand. He had no body! But how could he? As he had already reflected, his body was lying on the hospital bed … back wherever … dead. He heard a noise behind him. It sounded like some sort of deep growl. He turned quickly to see what, or who, had made the noise. Nothing! As he spun back to the front, there stood the most horrible creature he could image. All his life he had been enamored by horror stories. Never had he seen movie magic come up with anything so horrible. Standing a good eight feet tall, this "whatever" was the most horrible and mutilated specimen of a being he could imagine. Its flesh, or what Tim assumed was flesh, hung in long, putrid slabs. It seemed as though the chunks of flesh that hung in long ribbons were writhing like snakes. Each one had a head of its own. And as the thing stared at him, the heads of the snakes spewed some sort of putrid, yellow venom that burned Tim like acid. Once again, he struggled to scream, but no sound would come out. The creature spoke. Rather, it somehow relayed horrible sounding words into Tim's tortured mind. "I have a message for you from the Master. 'Welcome to hell, you miserable hated creature!' And because I have been appointed to make your orientation as horrible and painful as possible, I have been assigned a name for the task. I have been instructed to wear your name! So, you can just call me Tim" With that, the imp opened what must be its mouth and let out a horrible noise that was somewhere between a guttural laugh, and a scream. As he did, flaming, yellow bile spewed all over Tim, seeming to cook the flesh off his bones, if he had any (flesh or bones).

The vile creature continues. "In life, you stated that the stories about us were crap. You also said that heaven, God, and your new master were also baloney. You even denied the existence of our lovely home here. Well, I have been assigned to show you otherwise. And I can assure you that I will do my job well. My treatment of you will make you scream for God and His help. I will try as best I can to make you shriek even louder with each passing moment of eternity. That is how long I will torment you. And I will relish every act of torture. And there is no one who is interested in hearing your cries or in helping you in any way. You see, here, each person is totally wrapped up in his own set of things to screech about. There is no interest in 'helping his neighbor.' So scream away, you pitiful lost creature."

With that, he swung a huge, burning chain toward Tim's head (or where his head should be). Tim tried desperately to duck, but the chain wrapped around what now passed for a body: a burning mass of energy that was, in some way, connected to Tim's disembodied person. The chain glowed red hot, and Tim felt the fiery links bind him tight. The demon turned and began to drag Tim toward two huge gates that burned with a yellow and white flame. All around him, he could hear screams like nothing he had ever heard before. In his new understanding of what terror, pain, and fear were really all about, he knew this was his new eternity

The Welcome

Ed Is Welcomed Home

As the unlikely duo got closer to the colossal wall, Ed noticed it did not seem to have a gate or any sort of opening. It seemed to be a solid wall. He could see no signs of any kind of passageway that would allow one to pass through the wall. He assumed Asher would work some sort of feat that would suddenly reveal an opening that would allow both of them to pass to the other side of the wall and into whatever was on the other side. But to Ed's total amazement, Asher, without even hesitating, strolled right up to the face of the barrier and disappeared. He obviously had walked through the wall. To Ed's mind, still reasoning in earthly terms, that should be impossible. The wall looked like solid brass, or maybe gold, and stood at least one hundred feet tall. How thick was it? Ed had no idea. He stopped some ten feet from the wall, wondering what he was to do next. He waited for Asher to perhaps open a door from the inside. He was totally unprepared for what happened.

Suddenly, a huge head appeared, sticking through the wall. With a wide grin, Asher instructed Ed to just walk straight ahead, right through the wall. "Remember, you have a body made up of nothing but pure energy. You can pass right through." Ed began to move forward. It seemed utterly unnatural to keep walking right into a solid wall. And indeed it was, if one were still reasoning in biological terms.

When he reached the wall, he hesitated out of experience. But by moving ahead slowly, he found he could continue to walk forward, passing right through the substance of the wall. There was no resistance, only a somewhat odd feeling as he moved through whatever material made up the wall.

Ed's wonder at being able to walk through the wall was short lived by what he saw on the other side. His first gaze was into the distance. It was even more colossal than what he had seen on the other side of the wall. Never could he have imaged such a scene. Massive structures extended for what seemed forever. They were of all shapes and colors. Beyond that stood enormous mountains unlike any he had ever seen. They seemed to change colors as he gazed at them. They even seemed to change shape. Yet, he knew they were real. He supposed them to be more real than anything he had ever encountered on earth. The fronts were lined with massive columns, behind which he could see enormous, open doorways. They seemed to be made of the same material as the wall, yet in colors he had never seen. There were gardens and fountains everywhere. As he stared at what seemed to be thousands of different designs the water made as it sprayed up from the ponds, the water itself seemed to radiate some sort of energy. As he continued to watch, the energy seemed to saturate everything, even his very being. In fact, he seemed to be capable of extracting energy, or some sort of force, from everything here—the buildings, the fountains, and the flowers, all of it.

Everywhere, people were moving between the buildings, sitting next to the fountains; all seemed to be very busy. Those sitting alone by the ponds and fountains were reading. Where there was more than one person, they were talking excitedly about something. Occasionally, they would all laugh together. Then suddenly, they would all raise their hands to the sky and begin to sing. The very air was charged with what he knew was supernatural life energized by pure praise and worship.

His eyes were drawn to what was surrounding him. When he had passed through the wall, he had not observed anyone except Asher as he stood close. But now he was surrounded by beings, the like of which he had never seen. He instinctively knew they were glorified human beings, there to welcome him to his new home. How he knew that, he did not know. But it seemed that with every passing minute, his understanding and perception of all around him became clearer. He was being filled with a knowledge he could not understand: only accept. And it seemed that, as his understanding of his surroundings became more clear, so did his new energy body. He observed that the people who were surrounding him had bodies that were clearly visible.

Standing a short distance in front of him and moving toward him was what he believed to be the loveliest woman he had ever seen. She moved with an elegance he had never witnessed. She had long black hair. There was not one hair out of place, yet it hung naturally. Her completion was sort of golden, yet it literally radiated light. Her form was perfect, yet not seductive. Her eyes—he knew those eyes! Suddenly, he recognized her. This was his beloved Susan. The last time he had seen her, she was old, wracked with pain, nothing but skin and bones, and her hair only a few strands of white. She moved to him, and they embraced. Yet, it was not the embrace of a husband and wife. There was nothing sensual about the embrace. He had never experienced anything like it. This was a bonding of soul and spirit. It was a coming together of two members of the Royal Family of God. She did not call his name, but merely said, "Welcome home, beloved of the Lord!" She stepped back slightly, his hand in hers (he could feel it, but could not yet fully see his hand), and placed it in the hand of another glorious creature. As he looked into the eyes of this one, he at once recognized her. It was his mother. She also hugged him, and it was the same experience as with Susan. He did not call her "Mom," and she did not call him "Son." Once again, this was a silent bonding of supernatural beings that required no acknowledgment.

The next one to step before him certainly needed no introduction. Standing well over six feet by earth measurement, dark hair hanging to his shoulders, Ed knew his dad at once. He had the same deep-set eyes of his earthly Native American heritage. But he was, of course, totally different. At first he did not speak. He just looked deeply into Ed's very soul, relaying the same sense of power and love that had come from the others. He smiled. "Welcome home, Ed."

One by one, these glorious redeemed people came up to him and introduced themselves. In most cases, there was no need for an introduction. Family, friends, even casual acquaintances were all recognizable. Even those he had known only for a short time as a child. Susan stepped back up to him. "Ed, there is so much for you to see during your indoctrination to heaven. But we will meet again." Then, they were gone as quickly as they had appeared. They didn't vanish; they just moved on to the business at hand. Ed didn't have any idea what that was. He had assumed that the entire population of heaven would just be gathered around God's throne, singing and praising. So far, the only visible praise he had seen was from the few groups gathered at various ponds and fountains. Yet, he was aware that everything that existed here was, all at once and constantly, offering praise to the Master.

Suddenly, another question grasped his mind. *What about the others who—* Asher, once again, interrupted his question with the answer. "You are wondering if what you see here is all there is to heaven? If not, where are the millions upon millions of others who must have gone to heaven? The answer to your question is no! There are sections and levels of heaven without number. At points in your training, you will become a part of other sections or levels. And you will be able to freely move between them. There are many things yet to experience and learn. But it will all come in its place."

Asher motioned for him to follow him, and they proceeded down the unbelievably beautiful street, lined with huge buildings, parks, ponds with fountains, and ponds without fountains. Everywhere, people were busily going in and out. His curiosity was piqued. What could they possibly be doing that kept them moving around at such an excited pace?

Tim Is Welcomed Home

As the huge burning demon who laughingly demanded he be called "Tim" approached the white hot wall, he mercilessly dragged Tim (the recently deceased human) behind him. One end of the fiery chain was wrapped around his massive hand; the other seemed to disappear inside the essence of Tim's person. Tim's body was pure energy, and it seemed to drink up the flames all around him. Somehow, the chain had wrapped around the substance of his inner core and connected him to the demon's evil substance. Even the vile thoughts of the damned creature seemed to be transferred to Tim's soul. As they drew near the flaming wall, Tim writhed, trying to halt the forward progress. But the harder he struggled, the more he was dragged through the hot coals toward the terror that lay ahead. He had never known such agony, nor been so aware of all that was taking place around him. It was not just the pain but a sinister terror and a total sense of aloneness and despair.

The horrifying shape leading him disappeared into the flaming wall. Tim could see the chain also disappear into the wall. He wrestled with every ounce of his strength to avoid being dragged into the furnace, but to no avail. Suddenly, from the entrails of the wall, a horrid and mutated head appeared. It was the demon. He hurled curses at Tim, reminding him that to resist would only make things worse, which was okay with him. Then, with one powerful yank on the chain, Tim went airborne through the wall of molten horror and landed hard on the other side. What he saw next was far and beyond anything his terror-filled imagination had revealed so far.

Standing all around him was what he assumed had been, at some point, human beings. In a real sense, they still were, but now they were distorted beyond all recognition. They seemed to be composed of nothing but flame. They blazed, and from what he could make of their faces, they were in utter agony. Their shrieks were the most hideous sounds he had ever heard. Suddenly, they all seemed to look directly at him. Between their screams, they cursed him, seeming to blame him for their plight. In some strange way, he felt he could identify them as people who had been a part of his past. One he thought he recognized as his father. As he looked at the flaming spectacle, he remembered the beatings and sexual abuse he suffered as a child at the hands of this now pitiful creature. But it was as though the cruelty were actually taking place now, at this moment, and in addition to all the other horrors he was experiencing in his soul. His mind shrieked for it all to stop, but that only made it worse. The pain, the memories, and all the other emotions suffered by fallen humanity filled his total essence. As his gaze moved from one screaming, fiery creature to another, the hatred for all humanity, and especially for God, so filled him that it took on an existence of its own, totally consuming his being.

Then it was over! As suddenly as it had begun, all the pitiful, tortured creatures were gone. All that was left was Tim, the horrid imp, the indescribable pain, and what sounded like the sizzle of burning matter. Tim wept as best he could, and his demon guide laughed, if you could call it that.

Indoctrination for the Future

Ed Is Shown What His Training Will Be Like

ED AND ASHER MOVE DOWN the street between the massive structures that line both sides. People were everywhere, but none seem to be idle, without purpose. Some are in a hurry, moving alone. Others travel in groups. All have either books or strange-looking bags that seem to be full of something. But all seem to have a destination, often running up the steps leading into one of the buildings, or running down the steps, across the courtyard, and toward another building.

Ed still cannot get used to the divine look of each person. They all look perfect in every way. They wear what seems to be, in most cases, typical clothing. But their skin, their very countenance, is beyond description. They radiate with energy, so much so that the details of their bodies are hard to distinguish. He must continue to remind himself that these are not physical bodies but, rather, are made of pure spirit and energy. They are not limited by solid matter unless they wish to be, such as walking on the surface without passing right through it. Another question crosses Ed's mind. What is beneath them? Is it dirt, rocks, what? What makes up the surface of this place? Once again, as though reading his mind, Asher turns and instructs him to look down. As he did, he could suddenly see right into the ground, or whatever, beneath his feet. What he saw startled him so that he jumped. When he did, he rose some distance off the ground. Asher rose with him. Beneath where he had been standing, he could see the sky. At least, that is what it looked like. In other words, the sky—complete with stars, planets, galaxies, and so on—was not only above them in what he assumed was the sky of heaven, but space existed all around them. It was as though this entire heavenly dwelling place was suspended in the midst of the universe.

Both Ed and Asher settled back to the surface. "Come on!" Asher motioned for Ed to follow him as he moved toward one of the massive buildings. "Just wait 'til you see what's next!"

As they passed through the massive doors of one of the larger buildings, Ed gasped, catching his breath. Then he remembers that was impossible. Since his energy body had no lungs, he did not (and could not) breathe. But the site was overwhelming, to say the least, and it caused some sort of reaction. The walls of this huge, open room seemed to be at least several hundred yards long on three sides (by natural measurements). The room must have been well over one hundred feet tall. And on shelves that ran the total length and height, there were books. Books of every shape and every thickness. They did not look old and dusty, as one would think they might be. They looked as though they had just been printed. He walked over to a table where several books lay, some open, others closed. Asher stood beside him. "Sort of impressive, don't you think?" he mused.

"That's an understatement," was Ed's reply. "How many books are here?"

"More than you could imagine, even with your new imagining ability," said Asher. "And this is only one of these educational centers. But guess what? Your first task here is to digest all of them."

"You have got to be kidding." Ed almost laughed.

"Nope, and let me show you how." With that, Asher moved one of the thicker books closer to Ed. It was about twelve inches by fourteen inches and looked to be about several hundred pages thick. The title caught Ed's attention: *The Creator's Plan for His Royal Family.* Asher told Ed to lay his hands on the book. Ed was beginning to see the dim outline of his spiritual hands, so he complied. At once, the book began to glow, as did his hand. And in an instant, his mind was filled with more information than he had ever imagined could be contained by anyone. All that was inscribed in the book was transferred to his renewed and expanded mind, and he not only knew what was in the book, but could understand what every sentence said and meant. Ed suddenly began to comprehend what all creation was about. What the Creator had in mind. Asher explained. "These books are very special. And, as I have said, this is only one of the many repositories of information in this section of heaven. Remember, even though you are in the very beginning stages of your indoctrination, you are still a fully redeemed member of the Royal Family. Your mind has been opened to its intended capacity. You have the aptitude to integrate instantaneously the information contained in any of these books."

"But," Ed replied, "even at that, it will take years to go through all these books."

"Maybe so, if you were bound by time. But remember, time and eternity cannot coexist," Asher said. Ed let it go at that. "And," Asher continued, "it is usable and understandable as soon as it is assimilated. Let me show you something else. Do you like music?"

"Love it," was Ed's reply. They were standing in front of the most beautiful piano he had ever seen.

"Sit down," Asher said. Ed did, remembering how much trouble he had with trying to play something as simple as a jaw harp. Asher placed a piece of music in front of Ed. At the top of the sheet it read, *Handel's Messiah.* The heading of this particular score read, "Hallelujah Chorus." He had seen sheet music before, and it meant absolutely nothing to him. However, as he gazed at this piece, suddenly, he could not only read all the notes but could hear the score. It was as though he and the music notation had become one. He gently placed his hands of pure energy on the keyboard. He noticed that more of his hands and arms were now visible; there was a sort of a glow. He knew exactly what to do with his fingers, and the sound of this majestic music began to flow from the keys. His spirit and soul were lifted to new heights. The music mounted higher and higher, until Ed seemed to become one with the sounds of praise. He displayed all the emotion of an accomplished concert pianist. Before, he had not even been able to pick out "Chopsticks." But now, oh the glory he felt! Suddenly, there was singing and the sound of an orchestra all around him. And wow! What singing. He raised his head upward in spontaneous praise, and he saw from where the singing was coming. All around him, formed into a dome, were angels. And not just angels, but glorified humans, hands raised, all singing this magnificent piece of music. Seated all around him was what seemed to be a massive orchestra. As he arrived at the end of the score, Ed did not want to stop. He felt he could go on playing forever.

But Asher laid his hand on his shoulder. "We have much more to see."

As Ed brought the music to a resounding finale, he stood up from the piano stool. A tall young man approached him from the group that had been singing. He smiled at Ed. "My brother," he said, "I have seldom heard it played better." With that, he turned and walked off toward a group of people. As Ed and Asher moved toward the door of the building, Ed asked who this was. Asher looked down and smiled. "His name is George Frederick Handel."

Tim Is Shown What He Must Face

Tim the demon screeched at Tim the cursed, spewing green bile all over him. "Come on, you miserable scum. Just wait 'til you see what's next." Tim was too overwhelmed with pain and vile, evil emotions to move. The demon gave a jerk on the scalding chain binding them together. The body (or whatever it was that was now housing Tim's soul and spirit) literally bounced across the flaming floor of hell. The demon moved quickly ahead, giving a yank on the chain with each step. Tim looked like a flaming ball on the end of a giant burning rubber band, rolling and bouncing along, kicking up flaming embers with every bounce.

Suddenly, the scene changed. The flames and fiery glow began to lessen. The scene gave way to a deep, sickening gray color. Along each side of the trail, now more like hot molten ash, were what seemed to be large, old houses. They were all decayed and looked like haunted mansions Tim had seen in pictures on earth. The only difference was that they were on fire, yet they were not actually burning. It seemed that the scorching pain had diminished a bit. His mind was still being tortured by all the evil passions of fallen man. They overwhelmed him in nauseous waves. If he had a stomach, he would be vomiting with each wave. But he couldn't even have that bit of relief.

The monster mounted the steps leading to the entrance of one of the decrypted buildings, dragging Tim along behind. He shoved open one of the old, decaying doors. The inside of the building coughed out a putrid dust of death and corruption. The demon passed through the enormous double doors, Tim in tow. He paused in front of what appeared to be a large table, on which were stacked old moldy books. Snatching the chain, now just smoldering, he ordered Tim to stand upright in front of the desk. The demon picked up one of the books, handling it with what seemed to be reverence. He placed it in front of Tim. The title jumped out at him: *The Personal Diary of Jack the Ripper* was emblazed across the cover. Tim's tutor grabbed his still-burning hand (or where his hand should be) and slammed it down on the book. Instantly, all the horror, depravity, torture, and murder recorded in the book leaped into Tim's already tortured mind. At the speed of thought, Tim lived all the horrid events. He murdered, he tortured, he mutilated as though he actually was the monster who committed these acts.

Even before the visions and feelings left, the demon had slammed down another book in front of this tortured soul. This one: *Having Sex with an Infant*. As soon as he had read the title, the visions of what was contained inside filled his mind. It was not just knowledge. It was as though he was actually performing the things described in the book. And he was relishing in the experiences. But at the same time, he was disgusted with the scenes. He went from one set of "lived" perversions to another. Murder, bestiality, torture, mutilation: each one more enjoyable, yet horrible, than the last. Tim's entire person was wrapped in the worse sins possible for mankind. In his cursed mind, he was living and enjoying each one. Yet, at some level of his being, he hated each one. There was never a sense of fulfillment. With each experience, the desire for more horrible perversions grew.

Finally, he was dragged by his chain back outside. There, the full power of the pain returned. But in addition to the horrible, burning torture, his entire being was totally submersed in all the depravity possible to a fallen, cursed human being. Yet, the pain, images, and what seemed to be his actual activity in all the sin were so clear. He was performing what seemed to be hundreds of horrible acts of violence at once. There was never a climax, never a resolution, only continued acts of horror, over and over, with no satisfaction. And the most horrible of all? In the midst of all this horror, he could see in the background an image of Jesus Christ on the cross, paying for all he was going through. And the worse torture of all? At the same time he was experiencing all the horrors of sin, he was remembering in vivid detail every joke, every curse he had ever hurled at God and His plan. And he knew that it was too late for him to accept now what he had previously counted as foolishness.

His demon companion shot him a backward glance. "Just thought I would introduce you to that little show," he spewed. "Every so often, when I think you are having it too easy, I'll drag you down here for some more 'education.'"

Tim was vaguely aware of being dragged down the molten street. He wanted it all to just go black. Why couldn't he just fade into oblivion? Why did all this torture have to be so vivid and real? How long could he stand this? Suddenly, he remembered. This would be his plight throughout eternity. What was next?

Meeting with the Master

Ed Meets Jesus ... Face to Face

ED AND ASHER WALKED DOWN the street, now side by side, their destination unknown to Ed. As they moved along, Ed once again had to marvel at the texture and design of the street. It looked like gold, yet not totally. It had a bronze tint to it, as did all the structures. If he looked closely, he could see what seemed to be laid bricks in the street design. Yet, to his feet, now becoming more visible, it felt like the finest carpet. Soft, yet firm to the feel!

One thing he had noticed since he had passed through the wall was music. It seemed far in the background, almost unnoticeable. It was certainly not what was often referred to as elevator music back on earth. It was majestic, yet soothing. It was always there, in the distance, yet close. The only time he had noticed really loud music was ... well ... when he was the concert pianist.

They entered a huge open area, sort of like the first open area but immeasurably larger. To Ed, its width seemed to be that of several football fields, but it looked miles long. Flanking the area on two sides, Ed's right and left, were the most beautiful structures he had ever seen. They were even more spectacular than the ones he had already seen. He had no words to describe their design or colors. But it was the edifice at the far end of the plaza that really caught his eye. It looked like a city all its own. He could not see where it began or where it ended. And he could not see the top, because it rose all the way into the clouds. Until this moment, he had not noticed any clouds. The sky, if you could call it that, was bright but not blue like on earth. And he had already seen that if he looked close enough, he could see stars and planets in the sky, even though it was not dark, like night. But now, those clouds that hid the top of this massive structure were unlike anything he had seen. They were some kind of clouds; of that he was sure. He could see what looked like lightning flash from within the clouds. But the lightning bolts were golden. He was sure of that. There was no point in trying to describe them. They were beyond his ability to define.

Ed had observed they were walking alongside a river. He had been so taken by the buildings, he had barely noticed. But suddenly, it had his full attention. The water seemed to be flowing swiftly, but he could see no sign of movement, like should be normal with a flowing river. In the streams and rivers he had been accustomed to an earth, the various parts and currents could be seen. Here, it seemed as though the entire body of water (if that's what it was) moved together. Like so many things he saw here, his mind, even as clear and expanded as it had become, had no explanation for. The water was the brightest blue he had ever seen water to be. Yet, like everything else around here, it sort of shimmered with a golden tint.

As his eyes followed the river to its source, he saw that it flowed from a huge waterfall that erupted from the massive structure located at the far end of the clearing. He looked around for Asher. He would ask him about the building, clouds, and the river. He must know about this river! But the angel was gone. Quickly, Ed spun all the way around. He was totally alone. He did not feel alone. Yet, there was not another single person in all of this wide open area. Where was he? What was about to happen? He had the strangest, yet the most wonderful awareness of something. He had no idea what was causing this new sensation.

Suddenly, a solitary form materialized in the distance, seemingly from nowhere. The figure was moving toward him. Somehow, Ed recognized the form as a person. He was quite far off, toward the "city" located at the far end of the open area. Ed could barely make out his features, but he looked rather large and walked with a commanding gait, the likes of which he had never seen. He could tell that it wasn't Asher, but perhaps it was another angel. Maybe Asher had brought him as far as he was supposed to, and now the responsibility would pass to another. As the figure drew closer, Ed could see that it was not an angel, at least that is what his new, expanded mind was telling him.

The figure was now about what Ed would call fifty yards if he were on earth. He had no idea how space or time was measured here, except that Asher had said they didn't exist. It seemed that something was happening to him. He felt weak, yet sensed a strength unlike anything he had every experienced, even in this place. He wanted to fall down, prostrate on the ground—or pavement, or gold, or whatever it was. Yet, he wanted to explode with love and power. His eyes wanted to drop to the ground, yet they wanted to gaze full on and right into the eyes of the advancing figure.

As the man (he now knew it to be a man like no other he had ever seen) drew near, Ed took a chance and looked full into his face and locked eyes. Never, never, never could he have imaged what happened. It was as though the eyes of this one looked right down into his very consciousness. Even deeper: into his very spirit and essence as a created being. With that look, streamed love he knew he had never experienced, nor could in any way describe, even if he were given all of eternity to express what he felt. In a flash, Ed knew he was staring right into the eyes of the Redeemer, Jesus Christ, the King of the Universe, the One by whose very Word everything in the entire universe was held together.

Ed wondered why he did not just vaporize in the midst of the awesome power he sensed. Yet, he had never felt more alive. But that was not all. He was able to look right down into the soul of this one for and by whom all things were created. That should have been the encounter that would vaporize him, if anything could. Instead, his mind was suddenly filled with the wisdom of the ages. He had a new understanding of the cost paid that allowed him to be here, in this place, experiencing what he was experiencing. He grasped the realization of his station as a member of the Royal Family of God. A verse that he had heard his pastor preach about shortly before he arrived here burst into what was now his limitless understanding. "Beloved, now we are Children of God and it has not appeared as yet, what we shall be. We know that, when He appears, we shall be like Him, because we shall see Him as He is" (1 John 3:2 NIV). Ed somehow knew what he was experiencing now was only a "down payment" on what was yet to come. But even at that, it seemed as though his entire essence was being submerged in the Almighty Love that made up the very person and essence of Jesus Christ.

Jesus reached out and embraced him. "Welcome home, Ed." Somehow—in some way—he at once realized this would be the last time in all of eternity that he would be called by that name. In a flash, he was given an eternal name that had been known only to Jesus. Somehow, he comprehended that this symbol of identification had been assigned to him before the foundation of the world, when he had been "foreordained" in the mind of the Creator. He could not even pronounce it; he just knew it. Within that name was contained all he had ever been and all he would be as he served the King throughout eternity.

The divine consciousness continued. He knew that he was at this moment experiencing the richness of what another statement meant.

> For now we see in a mirror dimly, but then face to face; now I know in part, but then I shall know fully just as I also have been fully known. (1 Cor. 13:12 NASB)

Suddenly, the Savior was gone, and Asher once again stood by his side. "I'm sure you will agree that this face to face with the Master is the high point of your total existence. Your understanding and abilities have been launched ahead by what you may have before called 'light years.' This will become clearer as you move ahead in your training. Your basic indoctrination is about over. You will soon begin your training for your future here in the Royal Kingdom."

Ed was about to say something about the river. Once again, Asher seemed to read his questions before he could speak them. Asher held up one huge hand, indicating the time for that was not now. He was to learn later that this was the River of Life that flowed from the throne of God. It would have a very strategic function in bringing in the new age of God's Kingdom.

Asher concluded, "What you are about to experience will put, shall we say, a cap on this phase of what is in store for you. Hold on!"

Tim Meets Lucifer (or his rep)

As Tim bounced along, dragged by the demon and his chain, they suddenly stopped. Tim struggled to his feet. He was in the midst of a huge clearing. Wonder of wonders, he could see no fire. Only bleak landscape with black mountains, but no fire. Everywhere, there was putrid smoke, as though the fire had been suddenly extinguished. And the demon was gone. For the first time since arriving here, he was alone. The chain connecting him to the demon was gone. What was next? The pain was still there, as were the horrible images that invaded his mind. But that all seemed to be somewhat in the background.

From across the vast clearing, he saw a light. It was a glorious and welcome sight compared to what he had seen so far in this place. The light seemed to be getting closer, and brighter. Suddenly, it seemed to surround him. It was bright, oh so bright. Yet, it seemed ugly, sort of a dirty white. Then, from out of the light, stepped a figure.

Tim had never seen such a figure. It stood at least twenty feet tall. He was dressed like a warrior, maybe from the time of the Romans. At least, the pictures of Roman soldiers he had seen before were dressed sort of like this. But this was different. It looked like bolts of lightning were flashing from all over him. Not shooting out, but just circling him. Without a word, the being reached down and picked up Tim, holding him at arm's length and eye level. As Tim locked eyes with the warrior, he was filled with the most awful horror. He had already experienced fear that was beyond anything explainable, but not like this. He had a deep dread of all that was yet to come.

The being spoke. "Welcome to my home, worm! I am the representative of Lucifer, your Master. Such an insignificant waste of creation as you does not deserve a meeting with any of the Master's host higher than I. And I want to thank you for choosing us instead of … well … Him." His black eyes briefly shot up, as if making reference to something or someone above him. "I and my servants will make every attempt to make your stay as miserable as possible for as long as you are here, which," he smiled, "will be forever. I'm sure your stay will be a miserable one. But before we part, I would like to show you something."

Tim was suddenly standing in the most beautiful open place he had ever seen. It was totally different from everything he had been shown so far. All around him were giant buildings. They looked like they were made of brass, or maybe gold. And the sense of peace he felt was absolutely beyond words. Yet, he realized the peace was nothing he had; only something he sensed outside his person. All around him, he could see what looked like people. But they were so full of joy. Most of them carried books and moved in and out of the buildings. Scattered around were small ponds, most with fountains in the middle of them. Groups of people sat around the pools, either talking or reading from books they carried. Tim was elated. Could it be that he had paid for his sins? Is his time in hell over, and now he is being allowed into this place? Two people passed close by on their way to some place, obviously important. They were laughing and talking. He wanted to speak to them, find out where this place was. But they didn't even seem to notice he was there. They moved on. Tim decided he would walk up to one of the buildings, just to see what was inside. It sure looked different from the building he had just visited. But as he attempted to move forward, a horrible thing happened: he was suddenly tethered again by that infernal burning chain.

As quickly as he had arrived here, he was jerked back to the horrid place he had left. "No," he screamed. "Let me go back for just a while. Let me feel the peace that was there." All the pain, fear, and horror had suddenly returned. Looking down at him was the creature. "I just wanted you to see how horrible your life would be had been had you chosen to serve … Him." Once again, his dark eyes shot upward. "Can you just image living for all eternity in that sort of environment? But you chose us, and now you can enjoy the wonders of our beautiful home for all eternity."

Suddenly the scene changed. The demon who called himself Tim was back. He bent over and picked up the end of the burning chain. Tim, the cursed human, was once again bound to him, and all the pain and horror was back, and it seemed worse than before. Now, his mind was tormented with what he knew would have been had he not been so hardheaded and rejecting of all he heard about Jesus Christ. All was now totally hopeless. He knew that at the deepest level of his person. He was doomed.

A Vision of Destiny

Ed: Come Ride with Me!

ASHER HAD NO SOONER SAID the words, "Hold on," than the entire scene changed. Suddenly, they were suspended in what must be outer space. Ed looked in all directions: up, down, and from side to side. Everywhere he looked, there was nothing but space filled with fiery galaxies that whirled around, still being formed. Ed could see explosions that seemed to stretch from one end of the universe to the other. Ed started to ask Asher where they were, but once again, he seemed to anticipate his every question. "Consider the universe a giant globe," Asher suggested. Ed could at once picture it with a clarity that surprised him. It was as though he were now standing far off, viewing the universe from outside the universe, so to speak. He saw it as Asher had suggested: a giant transparent globe with the entire universe inside it. Asher continued. "Now, see yourself suspended at the very center of that globe." And just as suddenly, Ed and Asher were inside the globe, suspended at the very center. "Indeed, that is where you are. I want you to look at the entire universe with your new understanding. Open your mind to be filled with knowledge. What you will receive will help in your understanding of your place in the Father's grand scheme of all that is." And with that, he was gone!

Ed stood, or rather hovered, not seeming to be supported by anything, at the very center of all of creation. As he looked, he could see every corner of the universe. All the planets were crystal clear. He could see new planets, as they formed with mighty explosions. Then, they would come together with all the ingredients of a brand-new galaxy. Suddenly, he began to understand what it meant not to be constrained by time. He was watching the events from the perspective of eternity. As he watched, he began to see a new arrangement of order start to take place. The violence of the universe gradually began to be transformed into massive peace and order. He could see planets, as they become places where life could thrive. They were preparing to receive life. It would be forms of life that he could in no way imagine. But as he watched, he began to understand certain things recorded in God's Word. Terms such as "new heaven" and "new earth" took on meaning. Concepts and truths that he had never heard explained.

> When I consider Thy heavens, the work of Thy fingers, The moon and stars, which Thou hast ordained; What is man, that Thou dost take thought of him? And the son of man, that Thou dost care for him? Yet Thou hast made him a little lower than God. And dost crown him with glory and majesty! Thou dost make him to rule over the works of Thy hands; Thou hast put all things under his feet, All sheep and oxen; And also the beasts of the field, The birds of the heavens, and the fish of the sea, Whatever passes through the paths of the seas. (Psa. 8:3–6 NASB)

And,

> What is man, that thou rememberest him: Or the son of man, that thou art concerned about him? Thou hast made him for a little while lower than the angels; Thou hast crowned him with glory and honor, and hast appointed him over the works of Thy hands. For in subjecting all things to him, He left nothing that is not subject to him. But now we do not yet see all things subjected to him. But we do see Him who has been made for a little while lower than the angels, namely, Jesus, because of the suffering of death crowned with glory and honor, that by the grace of God He might taste death for everyone. (Heb. 2:6–9 NASB)

> and He has made us to be a kingdom, priests to His God
> and Father; to Him be the glory and the dominion forever
> and ever. Amen. (Rev. 1:6 NASB)

> And there will no longer be any curse; and the throne of
> God and of the Lamb shall be in it, and His bond-servants
> will serve Him; and they shall see His face, and His name
> shall be on their foreheads. (Rev. 22:3–4 NASB)

Ed had no idea how long he hung suspended there, watching eternity unfold before his eyes. Time was not a factor, so it did not matter. He knew that! He remembered what Asher had told him: "Time and eternity cannot coexist." Even with his vastly expanded capacity to understand the things of God and His Kingdom, there were just some concepts that were totally beyond his ability to handle, at least not yet.

He knew before many of the things he had envisioned could come into being, there was other work to do. Visions passed through his understanding. He saw phenomena that he would be involved in as a function of his place in the Royal Family. He knew he was just one of multiplied millions. Yet, his entire introduction had been as though he were the only one experiencing this introduction. He understood this to be a demonstration of the importance of each member of God's Family. A stimulating revelation passed by. Soon, there would be a massive battle for the earth and for those who were to be part of the family. All who were present with the Lord at the time of this battle would be in this Royal Army. He would have to learn to fight while on horseback. In his mortal life, he had owned several horses, so this would not be a problem. However, riding one in battle would be a new experience. But he now understood that such things would come easily.

Now, the time for what may be called "daydreaming" must be suspended. He must return to the training ground, for there was much to get ready for.

> I saw heaven standing open and there before me was a
> white horse, whose rider is called Faithful and True. With
> justice he judges and wages war. His eyes are like blazing
> fire, and on his head are many crowns. He has a name

written on him that no one knows but he himself. He is dressed in a robe dipped in blood, and his name is the Word of God. The armies of heaven were following him, riding on white horses and dressed in fine linen, white and clean. Coming out of his mouth is a sharp sword with which to strike down the nations. "He will rule them with an iron scepter." [a] He treads the winepress of the fury of the wrath of God Almighty. On his robe and on his thigh he has this name written: KING OF KINGS AND LORD OF LORDS. (Rev. 19:11–16 NIV)

Ed turned full circle, looking for the earth. There! He saw it! Right in the very center of the universe. The birthplace for God's Royal Family. He knew he still had mortal family down there. He knew that, depending on how long before the end of time and the second coming, he would have descendants born to his earthly family. In a moment of indescribable joy and sense of triumph, he shouted toward the small blue orb spinning below. He shouted to his descendants down through the ages: "Will you come ride with me?

Tim: Trapped in Darkness

Tim found himself back in the furnace. Once again, he was manacled to the demon. Being away from the pain for only a short span, and now for it to be fully reinstated, only made it seem worse. He was now in total torment, both in body and mind. He was constantly reminded that, even though he had no body, as such, the torment was as though he did. He could feel the burning and scorching through his hands and arms, as well as his torso and legs. But his face was where the pain seemed more severe. His eyes and lips felt as though they were melting. Even though he had no "equipment" that would allow him to breathe, he was forced to suck in the burning air that surrounded him. When he did that, it seemed like he was drinking in molten steel or something like that. There were no words to describe what he was experiencing. And all the while, the vile demon calling himself Tim laughed and occasionally gave a mighty jerk on the burning chain, which was once again binding them together.

Every new experience multiplied the agony. The last episode, the glimpse into what could have been his, was the most torturous. Even more so, because he knew he would never be able to experience it again. Oh, he would be aware of it. For all eternity, he would be aware of that glorious place, just out of reach. That would be part of his suffering.

As though reading his thoughts, the demon put his ugly and mutilated face right in Tim's face and screamed, the burning bile covering him. "Enough of this coddling, you miserable worm. It's time for me to tuck you in." They were standing at the very edge of what seemed to be a bottomless pit, filled with what looked like red and orange burning liquid. The demon literally jumped over the edge of where they were standing and into the burning caldron. Tim was jerked over the edge by the chain and followed the demon, screaming, into the flames. It seemed they fell forever through the roasting flames. Then suddenly, it all changed to total darkness. It was dark, but Tim knew the flames were still raging. He burned like never before, his mind seeming to relish each lick of the flames. It was as though he were suspended in midair, the molten furnace wrapping him in its arms. The demon spoke as he jerked the chain from around Tim. "I will be leaving you now," he spewed. "This will be your home from now on, through all eternity. You will be alone with your pain and your thoughts. But I promise I will look in on you ever so often. Enjoy!"

Tim began to scream and writhe in the torment. Even in all this, his mind was crystal clear. He could feel every evil desire known to fallen man. Yet, none could be satisfied. He knew his plight. He was not a mindless, tortured creature. He was a thinking being, fully aware of his fate and feeling each touch of the flames.

Suddenly—somehow—he was made aware of one more event that would cause him to be removed from this torment for a short time. At some time in eternity future, he would be suddenly yanked from this place to stand before the Creator. There, he would be asked to plead his case. Could he offer any reason why he should be removed from this torment? He must make his case on his own. There would be no one to represent him. He would have no advocate. Suddenly, he had a thought that seemed totally out of context with his present state. He would begin to build his case. He could tell about all the good things he had done on earth, although at this moment, he could think of not a single one. But perhaps he could make up some. Anything to get out of this place. But somewhere deep inside his tortured soul, he knew that any answer he gave would not be sufficient.

> Then I saw a great white throne and him who was seated on it. The earth and the heavens fled from his presence, and there was no place for them. And I saw the dead, great and small, standing before the throne, and books were opened. Another book was opened, which is the book of life. The dead were judged according to what they had done as recorded in the books. The sea gave up the dead that were in it, and death and Hades gave up the dead that were in them, and each person was judged according to what they had done. Then death and Hades were thrown into the lake of fire. The lake of fire is the second death. Anyone whose name was not found written in the book of life was thrown into the lake of fire. (Rev. 20:11–15 NIV)

Tim's name would not be found there!

Closing Words

As we bring our story to a close, there is one point I believe to be vital. We saw how Tim was born into some tough circumstances: the ghetto, a dysfunctional family, abuse, no instruction in basic human values. But that was not the reason he went to hell after death. The *only* reason was his rejection of Jesus Christ as his Savior. We saw Ed, born to a very functional family. He had a strong and credible family history. He ended up in heaven after death. His life situation had nothing to do with that, other than perhaps to provide a catalyst through which the gospel message had a better chance of being a part of his worldview. But that alone would not save him. He was in heaven solely because he accepted Jesus Christ as his Savior. If he had refused to do that, he would have been in hell with Tim. Or if Tim had accepted Christ, he would have been in heaven with Ed. It is vital to see that. Our eternal destiny is determined by not who we are but by what we become as a result of being born again. If you have never experienced this, I challenge you to read on, and read carefully. Below, I have presented a somewhat lengthy explanation of this process (as best as possible from our subjective position). For the one who does not wish to, shall we say, analyze the process, a simple commitment to Jesus as Lord and Savior will accomplish what needs to be done. Don't get me wrong. God has made it simple for us, because that is the way he intended. However, what takes place at rebirth is the most dynamic creation in existence. It is more profound than the creation of the entire universe. It is a lost and fallen human being becoming a newborn member of God's Royal Family.

If you are one who is more analytical about things that are hard to understand, I challenge you to study carefully what I present below. The desired result is the same: life throughout eternity, ruling and reigning with Jesus Christ.

Invitation to Join the Family

When we begin to talk about the born-again experience, we see a great deal of variance concerning just what is being referred to and how one experiences what is the most dynamic phenomena in existence. Getting it right is so vital that we'll simply allow the Word of God to lead us through the process.

At the outset, let me say that being born into God's Family doesn't take place purely as the result of some ritual, chanting some creed, or even going down front at the invitation some Sunday morning and praying the "sinner's prayer." Now, the rebirth experience could, and often does, take place during the performance of any of the above-mentioned things. But it's so vital to understand that it's not that act alone that can bring rebirth. No church can provide eternal life for you. No priest can admit you into God's Royal Family. And no amount of good works can get you any closer to heaven, and further away from hell, than can any creed or promise made to some church or even to God Himself.

Every act of receiving from God takes place as a partnership between the one seeking and the one giving. Some people try to do it themselves. They decide one day that it would be a good thing to get "saved." So, they ask Jesus to save them. However, it is done more out of a, "what if the scripture is right," attitude rather than from a desperate need. In other words, the asker considers that it would be better to be in good standing with God just in case there is truth to the story. Won't work that way!

Now, in presenting what follows, I do not intend to make the process seem more complex than it is. However, as I have already stated, it is the most profound event in the entire universe. Consider that what is happening is a spiritual birth more dynamic than one can imagine. Even more dynamic than your original human birth. A fallen human being, born into sin and a member of a dying race, is being supernaturally transferred from this fallen state to become a member of the divine Creator's own family. A spiritual creation is taking place that will affect the person's standing and future for all of eternity.

As you will see, it involves, first of all, action on God's part. The Holy Spirit, operating through some tragedy, some Christian friend's encouragement, or perhaps something some television preacher says, causes you to realize that you desperately need a relationship with the Creator. That is God's Spirit making known to you that He is anxious to receive you into His Royal Family. The next move is up to you. You must respond to this initiating move by God if anything is going to happen beyond this point. This response may be simply asking Him to move in your life, thereby accomplishing what you know you cannot accomplish yourself. It may involve confessing something that is in keeping with God's way to salvation, as revealed in His Word. Such a move on your part will ignite further action on the part of God.

The process will involve what may seem to an onlooker to be a sort of talking to one's self. As you confess, or ask, you are certainly asking of God. But there will also be a measure of what may be termed self-talk. You will send instructions to your spirit through your heart (subconscious mind). Your heart will, in turn, relay messages from the Holy Spirit back to your cognitive mind, where you make your decisions. Sounds somewhat strange! But God does it! Consider Genesis 1:26: "And God said, 'Let US make man in OUR image, after OUR likeness" (KJV; caps). That isn't just a matter of translation. The Hebrew word for God is *Eloim,* which is a plural noun and the term that refers to the Godhead—Father, Son, and Holy Spirit. What does that have to do with what we are saying here? It is proper, and often necessary, to have a conversation between my (conscious) mind, my heart (subconscious mind), and my spirit (the real me). Might want to be selective where this takes place. Some listening may think you've lost it.

Well, with that out of the way, what exactly does the scripture say in regard to this glorious and vital experience? We find all the ingredients in Romans 10:8–10. For our presentation here, each quote will be taken from the NIV. We will approach the verse in bites, examining each phase in detail. That will help you understand what has been said above.

The word is in you, in your mouth and in your heart ...

Here we see that the response to God's initial move on your behalf (call it conviction) begins with some action involving two elements of your human makeup. One is the mouth. The process requires for something to be spoken. Second, the heart must be involved. Words alone will not get it done. Words must be spoken, but they must involve some action by the heart in order for the words spoken to have any effect on your eternal destiny.

> That is, if you confess with your mouth, Jesus is Lord,
> and believe with your heart that God raised Him from
> the dead, you will be saved.

Can you see the progression here? The first act on your part must be a verbal statement from your mouth that you are proclaiming Jesus Christ as your Lord. This is more than a repeated affirmation based on what you have been told or what you have read. It must be a conscious decision made out of an act of desperation and determination.

The next step is a belief that transcends all logic. To the rational human mind, the idea of a person coming back from the dead is totally unrealistic. Based on all that we understand as natural, once a person has died, he remains dead. In fact, in a matter of hours, depending on the weather, his body will began to decompose. For the body to reanimate following death (especially after three days) would necessitate the reversal of a number of processes that begin at the moment of death. So, this portion of the equation that will result in the supernatural event we call being saved can't be the result of mind belief, drummed up faith, or a matter of mental programming. It must be something else altogether.
Consider this.

God, who sees the depth of our total person, hears that verbal/mental proclamation that Jesus is Lord. From that sincere human declaration, the Holy Spirit moves into action, placing a touch of faith within our human spirit. What kind of faith is this? We have stated that it can't be anything that's a product of the conscious mind or any other part of the soul. It must be from another source. We find a rather profound statement in Galatians 2:20 (NKJV):

> I have been crucified with Christ; and it's no longer I who
> live, but Christ lives in me; and the life which I now live
> in the flesh I live by faith in the Son of God ...

A good number of very reputable scholars state that the phrase, "by faith in the Son of God," should be read by the faith of the Son of God. Even if that isn't an absolute truth, a verse found in Hebrews. 11:1 provides evidence that this thing so shallowly referred to as faith can't be of purely human origin.

Now faith is the substance of things hoped for, the evidence of things not seen. (NIV)

The kind of belief that can be called biblical faith is a thing of substance. The Greek word states it as essence, or assurance, and something that sits under for support. It is a moving and vibrant force that can only emanate from the very person of God Himself. It cannot just be anything we conjure up from our human natures. It is for that reason that so many who have made pitiful attempts at rebirth through mouthing some creed or repeated prayer are woefully deceived. However, God is so full of grace, if He sees there is a sincere yearning on the part of the person to find peace with Him, He will move around all the often bad coaching and do whatever is necessary to bring that person into the Kingdom.

It is my sincere belief that at the moment of mouth confession, issuing forth from a determined mind desiring to know God, the Holy Spirit infuses his human spirit with a touch of the very faith of Jesus, or at least the same kind of faith Jesus has. At that moment, there ascends into the heart of the seeker a belief that cannot be questioned, and the person can no longer doubt that Jesus Christ is, indeed, alive. Now, the confession of this fact is filled with the power of faith, and it has creative power. It arises from deep inside the innermost parts of the person.

For it's with your heart that you believe and are justified ...(NIV)

In other words, it's the supernatural faith rising up in the heart that brings about justification, meaning that God pronounces you as though you had never sinned. All the wrongs you have done are placed under the blood of Jesus.

and it's with your mouth that you confess and are saved (NIV).

The word "saved" includes all that becomes available through this adoption into the Family of God. It includes all Christ bought at Calvary. That includes physical healing, financial blessing, and emotional health, on and on. But one point is vital. Each confession (specific need expressed) must be accompanied by an infusion of faith placed into the spirit and then rising up through the heart into the mind, and proclaimed out through the mouth with words. That can only be accomplished in keeping with the will of God concerning a particular situation or event. We cannot begin to confess things that are rooted in, and emanate from, our own sense of need (new cars, more money, and so on), unless that thing is in keeping with His will. In our present discussion, the thing needed is a rebirthing into the Family of God, and we know that this is God's prime will for every person on earth.

Let's see if we can tie the process into a simple workable whole.

It is vital to see that the process involves action! You cannot be born again from a passive mode. Can you see what I mean?

The first step in the process, following the conviction implanted by the Holy Spirit, is to confess with your mouth that Jesus is Lord. That is action alone. At this point, there may be nothing but a decision to proclaim Jesus as Lord. The only thing you may have at this moment is a sense of desperation. At this moment, you may have no idea what you mean. It may be more a general proclamation, arising, as stated, from a sense of desperate need rather than a personal statement. But it is action taken.

The next step involves action in the shape of an event performed by the Holy Spirit. He has already made known to you, through some means, your need for this relationship to be established. Now, He places a supernatural touch of the faith of Jesus into your human spirit. Result? A rising up of belief that Jesus is indeed alive. If you cannot in some strange internal way see Him alive, the former confession is mute and rather pointless. You must perceive Him alive, not from the position of understanding, nor even mere acceptance of the fact. Rather, it must be the result of revelation that transcends cognitive activity. This produces supernatural faith that energizes belief. His faith and your resultant belief bind together in the heart, and you can no longer doubt that Jesus is presently alive and that He is not just Lord, but *your* Lord! Remember, this is in no way based on reason! When you hear some former drug addict tell how, at the moment he actively received Jesus as his Savior the addition left at once, it is because of this depth of revelation. That is not to say that unless you have a similar experience your rebirth is unreal. But it does seem that when there is a deeper level of sin, and the rebirth is profound, the change is also profound.

How now does your own belief (or faith) rise up to the level of the cognitive mind?

Faith comes by hearing, and hearing by the Word of Christ. (Rom. 10:17 NKJV)

Perhaps a more clear translation, which stays absolutely true to the verse, is, "Faith comes by hearing the Word spoken by Christ." So, as the infusion of faith enters your spirit, and that Faith of Christ passes through your heart into your mind, you can *hear* the Word of Christ, and now, unexplainable faith (belief with substance) rises up in your mind. You do not understand it, and you cannot explain it; it is just there.

The last element in this glorious process is a new confession, spoken not out of a decision of the mind but from the very depths of the innermost being. The result of this act brings into existence an additional depth of faith. There is now absolute confidence that what God has said that He would do, *has been done*! At that point, the, "Spirit Himself bears witness with our spirit that we are the children of God" (Romans 8:16 NKJV).

If you have never before experienced this so great Salvation, I urge you to proceed as has been laid out in these pages. However, one thing not directly brought into the process was the importance that *you expect* God to respond to your confession exactly as He has said He would. Concerning the asking of anything from God, James 1:7 (NKJV) proclaims, "But let him ask in faith without any doubting, for the one who doubts is like the surf of the sea driving and tossed by the wind. For let not that man expect that he will receive anything from the Lord."

One thing is absolutely sure. If any person cries out to God and fully expects Him to respond according to His will and His Word, that person can be sure he or she will receive from God what they ask.

I close by simply saying that if you have taken the action above, ***Welcome to the Family!***